J. N. (John Newton) Stearns

Merry's Book of Tales and Stories

J. N. (John Newton) Stearns

**Merry's Book of Tales and Stories**

ISBN/EAN: 9783743324251

Manufactured in Europe, USA, Canada, Australia, Japa

Cover: Foto ©Andreas Hilbeck / pixelio.de

Manufactured and distributed by brebook publishing software
(www.brebook.com)

J. N. (John Newton) Stearns

**Merry's Book of Tales and Stories**

# MERRY'S BOOK

OF

# TALES AND STORIES.

.

EDITED BY
UNCLE MERRY.

NEW-YORK:
H. DAYTON, No. 36 HOWARD STREET.
INDIANAPOLIS, IND. : ASHER & CO.
1860.

J. J. REED, PRINTER & STEREOTYPER,
43 & 45 Centre Street.

# CONTENTS.

# ENGRAVINGS.

# PREFACE.

"TRUTH is stranger than fiction." And true stories if well told, are not only better and more instructive, but more entertaining than fictitious ones. We do not mean to say that all the stories in this volume are true in all their details ; but they are true in this, that they speak truly of the habits and feelings of children and youth, and illustrate truly the temptations and dangers to which they are exposed, and the duties they are required to perform, or they relate some interesting fact in natural history. We think that no story can be truly amusing even which has not some good lesson in it—which does not justly represent some peculiar aspect of our life, some trait of character, some natural incident of human history, or some fact in the history and habits of the animal creation. We are quite sure that our young friends will agree with us in this ; and that any of them would much prefer a plain tale of truth to the most glowing pictures of fairies and

they have seen, without **the trouble and** expense **of**
visiting them in **person.** This is a very profitable and
interesting kind of reading, and one that **never tires.**
It affords a great variety of information and pleasure.
We learn geography from the description of the coun-
tries, **and the** seas, the rivers, the lakes, and the moun-
**tains,** which the traveler explores. We learn history
from his accounts of the country and its people—natural history from his description of the animals, birds,
&c.—botany from his **account of the trees, and** plants,
and flowers, **and so on**—adding **to all our stores of**
knowledge, **in** proportion **as our traveler is** particular
and accurate in describing all he sees. Travels, voyages, and adventures, are always found to be interesting and acceptable to the young. We trust they will
**be pleased with what we have given them here. We**
know with what great **delight and profit the whole**
Merry family followed Peter Parley **in** his "Balloon
Travels," visiting some of the most prominent and interesting places in the world, and becoming acquainted
with a great many things **they had** never heard of **be-**
fore. And we know how sorry they **were when the**
travels came to an end. We have **often wished we**
had a balloon of our own, that we might take them **all**
out on another excursion in some of the unvisited re-

gions of the earth. As soon as we can find one that can be safely trusted to carry so large and precious a family, we shall send out our invitations far and wide, and a glorious time we will have. Till then, we shall do all we can to supply the place of a personal visit, by giving the best that we can find of the travels and voyages of others—that is to say, those best adapted to the tastes and capacities of young persons.

And now, a word of advice, in reading travels and voyages. Always endeavor to put yourself in the place of the traveler. Make yourself fully acquainted with his descriptions, so that you can bring distinctly before your mind the places he visits. Take your maps, and trace out his course, and find all the places he mentions. Recollect all you have ever read about them before. Imagine yourself in the place of the writer ; enter into his feelings, and then you will be prepared to understand all he says, to remember it, and profit by it. And then too you will derive the greatest possible pleasure from all that he is disposed to tell you. This is particularly necessary in the reading of personal adventures, feats of daring and danger, hair-breadth escapes, &c. It is impossible fully to understand and appreciate them, without, for the time we are reading them, putting ourselves, as it were, in the place of him who writes or relates them.

---

## THE BIRTH-DAY PARTY.

FAR from the city and the "busy haunts of men,"
in the little village of B——, lived Annie Cameron, a blithe, gay child, who had never as yet
known sorrow, or shed a tear for aught else than
perchance for the committal of some slight fault, or
over the death of some antiquated pet. She with
her mother lived in a rose-embowered cottage, where

the brilliant humming-bird ever was welcome, and where the summer breezes gently shook the leaves or played with Annie's long curling hair, and any one that had seen her for the first time when I did, would have thought that the wind used it as a plaything pretty often.

She had been out with a party of little friends gathering strawberries, and many a stain here and there betrayed her occupation, her cheeks doing their best to rival the rich color of the fruit. Her dress was caught up, not ungracefully, but certainly unknowingly, by a piece of briar-rose which had clung to her during her ramble. Her long curls were blown back from her face in wild confusion, while a wreath of field flowers, strung together with the united taste of the strawberry party, held her hair in unwilling bondage.

I had arrived at B—— that afternoon on a visit to my mother's old friend, Mrs. Cameron, and I had been listening to a parent's description of her only child just as the door flew open, and in rushed the whole flock eager to tell of their frolic and adventures. All stopped at the sight of a stranger except Annie, who sprang forward to her mother, throwing a large bouquet into her lap, and then turning to me said, "I suppose as you are mamma's friend, you are mine, too, are you not?" and a smiling assent soon made us as familiar as old acquaintances.

Annie introduced many of her little companions

to me, and I was soon in earnest conversation with Lizzie and Herbert Gray, Julia Lunt, James Ward, and I do not know how many others, each anxious to tell of the afternoon's fun in his own words. Lizzie Gray said she knew where all the finest strawberries that her brother had picked were to be found, and she laughingly pointed to a little basket made of oak leaves, well filled with the largest and reddest wood-strawberries I have ever seen. The basket bore on it the name of Annie, pricked in the leaves with a pin, and she soon claimed her property.

The little party now separated, and we were left to ourselves. Tea was served, and Annie seating herself at the head of the table, presided as demurely as an old housekeeper, and when we had left the table and drawn to the window to watch the glowing sunset, she rang the bell, and the neat maidservant brought her in a little tub, mop, and napkin, with which she carefully washed and wiped the silver tea-set, and put it carefully away—not till then did she join us at the window.

Mrs. Cameron and I talked about old times, and she told me of her intimacy with my mother when a girl. She told me of their studies and pleasures, of their duties and amusements ; her mother combined the useful with the agreeable in the education of her children, and rigidly insisted upon duty before pleasure. She thought that "all work and no play," and "all play and no work," were equally

wrong, and would surely "make Jack a dull boy."
Among others of her childish pleasures, Mrs. Cameron mentioned a little party her mother once gave,
in which all her young friends were dressed in the
costume of some country, each character telling
something of her presumed home, of its situation,
climate, habits, &c., thus giving a series of geo-
graphical lessons, at the same time instructive and
amusing. We were highly entertained by Mrs.
Cameron's account, and Annie said, "Oh! mamma,
why not let me have a little party on my birth-day,
and let us dress in costume, too, it will be so new
and interesting to us all, and you know next week
vacation begins, so that it shall not interfere with
our lessons ; I will not even mention it till then, and
oh, what fun we should have ! Minnie, plead with
and for me, won't you ?" Who can resist a request
from an only child, when the request is reasonable
and proper, and when the bright eyes and happy
face of that only child are looking so earnestly into
yours ? Not Mrs. Cameron certainly, for though
like her mother rigid in enforcing duty, she likewise
delighted in giving pleasure.

The assent was given, and Annie performed a pi-
rouette, which soon brought her panting to her seat.
" Annie," said her mother, " I have several condi-
tions to make as regards this little party. 1st.
Nothing new shall be bought for any dress. I do
not like useless or frivolous expense. 2dly. Your

characters shall all be kept secret, and I will have you announced as you enter the room. 3dly. The party shall commence and close early. I do not wish to be reproached by heavy eyes and aching heads on the morrow. 4thly. Your birth-day comes on Saturday, and as I do not wish to have your Sunday's duties mingled with the thoughts of your pleasure, we will postpone the party until the following Tuesday. Now to bed, and sleep soundly." And with a good-night kiss was Annie off to dream of strawberry parties and birth-day parties until morning.

The few days before vacation flew rapidly by, and studying hard and sewing more industriously than ever, the promised pleasure only made her the more desirous of deserving it, and her lips conned their lessons, and her needle flew in and out, taking rapid but small stitches.

Vacation came, and the very day it began, Annie and I wrote about thirty invitations, in which all the parents of the invited children were begged to be present, and soon Annie's birth-day party was the talk and anticipation of the village. The young people met but little during the week of preparation. Youthful faces were full of bright thought, and little fingers were busy in shaping and sewing. Dark closets were ransacked, and old-fashioned garments again saw the light. In the search, missing and lost articles were found, and everything was dragged out, and scanned, and **discussed, and** ingenuity was taxed to **turn** every thing to account **for** the eventful day.

Mrs. Cameron, Annie, **and** I, worked like beavers. Herbert Gray came several times during the week, and he and Annie had evidently some plan together **of** which I knew nothing, nor could I learn any**thing.** I asked but once, and for answer received a roguish laugh from Annie, as she tantalized me with my ignorance. Mrs. Cameron was, however, **soon** admitted to be one in the secret, for unless her mother **was consulted, Annie** would not **think any** plan good, **or likely to** succeed.

The evening came. Mrs. Cameron and **I** lighted **the** lamps and candles, wiped away every stray grain of dust, arranged garden flowers in the parlor, **and** field flowers on the supper table. We then gave **one** last **look at Annie as she stood ready dress**ed for her first party, and then went down to receive **the** company, for we already heard voices in the hall.

The parents all arrived first as requested, in order that even the first comers might find spectators awaiting them.

A quarter **of** an hour elapsed, and then, after several rings **at the** door-bell, a smothered laugh, **and** a good deal of ohing and ahing, the door was thrown open, and one by one, as they were announced, in came the expected characters.

A graceful figure, draped in black gauze, entered

the door.  Her head was covered with a long veil
spangled with silver stars, and a crescent moon
formed the front of the crown which encircled her
brow.   Upon one shoulder sparkled a diamond star,
with a silver anchor beneath it.   On the other, beneath gauzy pink clouds, shone an equally liquid
star.   All this I saw at a glance, as the figure moved sedately across the room : and I knew that the
dark-eyed Lizzie Gray personated "Night."     I

knew that the mariner's hope and guide the "North
Star," and Venus, the "Evening Star," shone in
bright rivalry on her shoulders.

After her, in rapid succession, came a flower-girl presenting a fragrant bouquet to all ; a gleaner with an apron-full of wheat; and a sailor-boy, who looked as ruddy as an old sea-captain. We waited a moment, and then the door opened again, and a voice, which I knew to be that of James Ward, announced "an indigent individual who received no invitation, Rolla Gray, Esq. ;" and in walked the great Newfoundland on his hind legs, with a white cap and apron on, looking the cook to perfection. We had a hearty laugh at his appearance, and dismissed him to his proper place, the kitchen, where due attention was paid to his appetite. Visitors were now constantly arriving, and many and various were the costumes ; but not to make my story too long, I will only tell of the most striking.

Julia Lunt, with powdered hair and a rich brocade dress, high-heeled shoes, a short waist, a long train, and one or two little black patches upon her face, made an excellent and graceful court beauty. Ellen Morris was a tiny Red Riding Hood, with a most tempting display of cheese-cakes, and a little pat of butter, which she had herself churned for Mrs. Cameron. The announcing of "The Spoiled Child" attracted our attention, and James Ward came in. His hair was in twenty snarls, his face was streaked with dirt, and his eyes red with apparent weeping. He had a half-eaten apple in one hand, and a stick of candy in the other. Behind him came his nurse

(Ellen Ward) trying to coax him to be dressed ; and soon after his mother (Laura Lunt), alarmed by his angry cries, came running in with the sugar-bowl. Nothing, however, would do : he would neither be appeased or dressed ; and finally, in a paroxism of passion, was taken out of the room, and did not return as " The Spoiled Child."

This little scene amused us very much : but I thought there were one or two mothers who looked rather conscious, and they must have learned a lesson that evening. When James came back, little Ellen jumped up, and began—" Fy !

> " Not wish to be washed !
> Not wish to be clean !
> But rather go dirty !
> Not fit to bo seen !"

Which sent James, apparently overcome with shame, into a corner.

I was beginning to wonder where Annie could be, and was upon the point of asking for her, when a voice, weak from age, but very sweet, was heard singing :—

> " Pity the sorrows of a poor old man
> Whose trembling limbs have borne him to your door,
> Whose days are dwindled to tho shortest span,
> Oh ! give relief, and Heaven will bless your store."

We all ran to the window, and throwing open the blinds, saw standing in the moonlight an old man bent with age, his gray head uncovered, and his tot-

tering form supported by a little girl, whose tatter-
ed, though clean dress, and smoothed hair bespoke
at once her poverty, and a desire to make the best
of her little all.

The two, seeing the sympathizing looks of all,
now approached the window, and on Mrs. Cameron's
asking them if they did not sing together, they began the following :—

Oh ladies bright and fair,
Of gentle mien and air,
Who know nor grief nor care,
    **Take** pity !
**We ask but a slight gift,**
**Oh give a helping** lift,
Down Sorrow's stream we drift,
    Oh hear our dity !

'Tis good from your full measure
Of fortune and of treasure,
**To give relief and pleasure**
    **To the poor !**
Then list unto our prayer,
Some answer through the air,
Will mount to realms more fair,
    Be sure !

The blended voices ceased ; and all hearts were
touched, and purses opened, and many were the
bright pieces that found their way into the box
passed round by the little girl.

We counted the money ; there were **three dollars**
and forty-**two** cents ! The grateful **singers bowed**
low, and methought, as they gave thanks, **the** old

man's form looked less bent, his eye more piercing.
Methought the little girl looked more gay, and—I
started—was I mistaken? No! for, throwing
away false hair, rags, staff, and all but the money
box, the beggars (Herbert Gray and Annie Cameron)
stood revealed in Scotch costume. Nothing was
wanting, the tartan and the plaid, the heron plume
and the maiden snood, Scotland's thistle and the
kilt—all were there; and the bright and happy
couple were the hero and heroine of the evening.

All were now assembled; and gaily flew the
hours, dancing, singing, and music all lent their
aid. The supper table was loaded with the good
things of this world, and the jellies and candied
fruits, cakes, and ices, all spoke of Mrs. Cameron's
housely hand. Every thing had been made at home.

The mammoth bouquet in the middle of the
table was the offering of the poor children of the
village, who, on the next day, all received some of
the evening's entertainment.

The money collected was bestowed upon a suffering and needy woman, whom Mrs. Cameron well
knew as a hard-working and worthy object for relief,
and more than the mere partakers in it enjoyed the
remembrance of Annie Cameron's birth-day party.

## "COMING THROUGH THE HAY."

HARLIE and the boys had **been doing** their utmost to finish the job, and **get** in all the hay before dark, **as they were** to have the next day for holiday. The mea-dow was well-nigh cleared. One or two **loads** more would take it all, and yet the sun was **a full** hour high.

"We'll do it, Charlie," said William to his bro-ther, "and have ample time to get all our fixing ready this evening."

"You may as well say it is done already," replied Charles, "for there is time enough, and a will. So we will have to-morrow for a party to the Lake."

"That we will," cried Fanny, rushing out from behind the great tree, where she had paused a mo-ment **to** learn what her cousins were so earnestly talking about, as they stopped in their work and leaned **upon** their rakes **for a** single moment— "That **we** will, Coz, and **Mary**, and Lucy, and two **or** three more of the girls, will be here soon to **have a little** consultation about the matter."

"I am afraid," said Charles, keeping steadily at work while he talked, "you will only hinder our work, so that we shall not finish it up to-night, and so shall not be able to go at all."

"So ho!" exclaimed Fan, with a wild, musical

laugh, that was peculiar to her, "if we hinder you a bit, we will help you more. We will turn to, all of us, and toss, rake, or pitch; and if we three girls don't beat any three of you boys, we will **pay the forfeit, that's all."**

Mary and Lucy now came up, with two or **three** more of the **same sort.**

At **the same** moment, the wagons returned **from the barn, and the boys were** all **on the** ground. **Discussion** ran high. **There** was no moderator, **no rules of** debate. Two, three, **and** four would speak **at the** same time, while laughter and joke filled up all the gaps.

After a time William succeeded in **getting some-**thing like order, **so as to be heard.** The plan **was** all laid **out, and a part** in the arrangements assigned **to** each one, to which **each** and all assented. **There** were lots of things to be done. Cakes, and pies, and fruits, and all the *et cetera*, were to be got ready.

" It will be midnight before we get through **with** all these preparations," **said Charles.** " Now **hurry** away, all **of** you, and let us get in the rest of the hay."

" We'll have a bit of dance first," said Fanny, with a mischievous laugh. " Here, George, out with your flageolet, and blow away briskly. We have no time to lose."

Suiting the action to the word, she seized **Charles** by the hand, threw down his rake, **and drew him** under the shade of the great tree.

" So be it," cried two or three of the boys, **and** choosing each his partner, soon filled up the set.

Merrily, merrily they tripped the light fantastic, as if there were no work to be done, no preparations for the morrow to be made. "Begone, dull care," seemed to smile on every face, and speak from every eye. Meanwhile, some who did not dance did something else—made love under the trees, as Ben and Susy are doing, or looked on with downright sympathy on the fun, but with a grave wish that the hay was in, as Jerry, that old fellow on the left, is doing, and with a sober thought of the cakes and pies, as prudent Charlotte is doing on the right.

Well, the dance came to an end, and the day was coming to an end too, and Charlie and William sprang to their rakes.

"Come, boys, now set to with a will," exclaimed old Jerry. "Only twenty minutes to sundown, and two good loads to get in yet."

Where there's a will, there's a way. Oh! what marvels of work were done in those twenty minutes! There was a will in the work, and all worked to that one will. The girls took hold, as if they knew how. They raked the hay in heaps, they carried it in their arms, for want of forks, and then they mounted the wagons, and spread and pressed the hay, in the best possible style. They worked like men, as Jerry said, evidently intending a first-rate compliment. But Fanny repudiated the comparison, as unworthy of her sex. The women, she said, could and would always beat the men, at any work they might undertake.    She therefore claimed that they worked like girls, and that was enough.    Jerry yielded the point very gracefully, and declared he would like to hire a dozen such hands to help him, at the next haying. Fan offered her services, and those of Susy and Mary, free gratis for nothing, and begged he would give them one day's notice, when he wanted them.

When the sun went down, the last load of hay was stowed away in the loft, and the boys were leading the horses to the brook.

## PICNICS.

JUNE is the very season for Picnics. Everywhere men, women and children, are planning and executing excursions. Strawberries, cream, nuts, crackers, cakes, lemons, ice, and all the et ceteras of good eating, are in pressing demand. Baskets, boxes and bags are enjoying unwonted popularity. Omnibuses, with feathers and flags for the horses ; steamboats with streamers, and wagons, carts, and nondescript vehicles of every form and size, are up for daily charter, and active competition ; and groves, orchards,

dells, glens and copses are sedulously explored, sur-
veyed and discussed, as if millions were about to be
staked in hopeful speculation. Then, as to lawns,
laces, tissues, muslins, ribbons, flowers, jewels, and
all that sort of thing ; time and words would fail,
should we essay to speak of them. But of the hu-
manities of the scene we may speak freely and know-
ingly. Of these there are, as usual, every variety,
from the octogenarian to the infant of days, white
heads, gray heads, black heads, brown heads, red
heads, auburn heads, yellow heads, straw heads,
round heads, flat heads, long heads and all sorts and
sizes of heads. There is beauty and its opposites of
all degrees and shades. There are simplicity and
affectation, pride and grace, wisdom and folly, fun
and pleasure, and all the countless phases and forms
of character and condition, all huddled and jostled
together, like the shines and shades in a kaleidescope,
and producing, to the observant eye, just such phan-
tasmagorean shapes and changes. It would be a
study for a philosopher. But, being no philosopher,
I will let that pass, and attend to the more palpable
and material part of the scene, the outside enjoyment,
which is all that I can reach at present.

"The Grove" is a little paradise of a place, and
is now in its best possible condition. The trees are
in all the leafy freshness and blossom of June. The
grass, over which the scythe was passed a few days
ago, is starting into new life, as soft and smooth as

a carpet of velvet. The walks are all clean, as if swept this morning for the occasion. The arbors and rustic seats are gay with vines and flowers.

THE VINE ARBOR.

The birds are full of song and sweetness, and wholly unable to repress their exuberant joy, in view of the rich repast of crumbs of which they are evidently expectant, and which they seem perfectly willing to pay for beforehand, by notes which require no endorsing, and which are always and everywhere current. The sky is clear and cloudless, though for the most part hidden from view by the luxuriant foliage of the grove. The air is as delicious as the cool sea from which it comes, and the gardens of roses and acres of honeysuckles, over which it has passed, can make it. The company assembled are all pleased with themselves, with each other, with the day, the grove, and the occasion, and nothing seems wanting to complete their enjoyment.

In a sweet little dell, overhung with heavy and fragrant foliage, a long low table has been placed. It is loaded with all the luxuries, and many of the substantials of the season, and arranged with exquisite taste by hands formed only for the graceful and beautiful. Flowers and greens are sweetly interspersed with fruits and other dainties, and it is difficult to tell whether the eye, the smell, or the taste, are most to be regaled.

While this is being prepared, let us walk over the grounds and witness the various kinds of enjoyments which, in this simple way, are provided for so many. Here is a group of gay children playing at graces. Their hats are carefully tied up in the branches of the young saplings that nestle under the shadows of the larger trees. The many-colored hoops fly back and forth with a beautiful motion, and the attitude and action of the young performers are exceedingly graceful, picturesque, and well entitle this sport to the name by which it is called. Here we come to a party of boys playing ball ; this open ground, outside the grove, is just the place for it, and the sport is

active, manly, and full of spirit, just adapted to de-
velop a quick eye, a ready action, celerity of movement, alertness, precision, and an easy adaptation to
unexpected emergencies. Health and happiness to

THE SWING.

you, boys, keep the ball in motion, while we pass on
to this merry company of butterflies on the shady
knoll yonder. Merry, indeed, and happy as larks,

playing hide and seek among the thick undergrowth,
and behind the aged trees; and here, in this quiet
dell, is a young gipsy, telling fortunes, and keeping
all the little ones around her in high glee, by the
amusing and grotesque pictures she draws of their
future. See at what a dizzy height that brave girl
is swinging; do not fear for her, the rope is strong
and well secured in the crotches of two stout trees.
The seat is a firm one, and a strong strap is passed
round in front, so that she cannot fall out. Let the
pendulum vibrate, with its living weight at the bottom; so life itself vibrates between the extremes of
joy and sorrow, then wanes and stops, and gives way
to another, and another, and another. Heigho!
that thought has too much shadow for this time and
place, let us pass into the sunshine again. Here is
a boy with a burning glass, trying to set fire to the
green grass, but it won't even smoke; he wishes he
had a little powder, but that, surely, would be out
of place in a picnic. Here is a bright company, amusing themselves with a camera obscura, on which they
are delighted to see all the groups and divisions of
their gay party, their various movements, crossing
and recrossing, their endless changes of position.
"Aha!" says Charlie, "I do believe the whole grove
and everybody in it, is shut up in that little box. I
wish I could look inside."

Well done, Charlie, look in and learn, meanwhile
we pass on to—what is this? a throne! yes, and a

queen, and who knows how many lords and ladies,
knights and fairies, nymphs, floras, and all sorts of

THE MAY QUEEN.

bright and beautiful witches. What does this mean ?
Hark, the trumpet sounds, summoning all the queen's
loyal subjects to attend her coronation ; and lo ! they
come, flying in from all directions. The swings are
vacant, the grace hoops are hung on the trees, the
ball is no longer in motion, the camera is painting
the scene, with no one near to admire it, and all the
world is here. The queen ascends the throne, kneeling on the lower step, as she goes up, to receive her
crown of flowers. She addresses to her subjects a
hope that they will enjoy and improve the day, so
that the memory of it will be all sunshine and flowers. They reply in a sweet song to the " queen of
flowers," which makes the grove ring and the distant
hills echo, and startle all the birds to renew their
songs. The queen thanks them for their kind wishes, invites them to the feast, and leads the way.
We follow and partake ; but to describe that feast,
with its innocent mirth, its sweet effect upon heart
and manners, its refining influence upon the rude,
its harmonizing influence upon persons of different
tastes and habits, and its generous interchange of
kindly feelings between those in different ranks, who
seldom meet elsewhere,—is more than we shall attempt. We leave it to be imagined, or rather to be
tried. Try it, parents ; try it, sabbath schools ; try
it, neighborhoods ; you will find it a most happy blen-
ding of *utile cum dulce,* in which the useful shall be
altogether sweet, and the sweet altogether useful.

## THE BRIGHT SHILLING.

*"It is more blessed to give than to receive."*

"COME, Clara and Minnie, put up your dolls, dears ; it's getting quite dark, and only wants ten minutes to bed-time," said Mrs. Anderson to her children, two merry little creatures of five and seven years old. The gentle Minnie obeyed the summons at once, saying to her sister, who seemed not to hear it, "Perhaps mamma will tell us a story, Clara, before we go to bed, if we tidy up quickly."

"It must be a very short one, darling," replied mamma.

"And a true one, please, ma," added Clara ; and in a few moments the two little ones had seated themselves on a large stool, at their mother's feet, and nestled their heads in her lap, while she related as follows :—

"One day, while papa and I were staying in New York, last autumn, at Mrs. Steven's, I was walking through one of the narrow streets, with her little Emily (who is about your age, Minnie), by my side, when we saw a thin-faced, sorrowful-looking child, sitting on a doorstep, and binding a pair of shoes, stopping every now and then to wipe away the tears from her red and swollen eyes.

" 'What's the matter, dear ?' I asked.

"The little girl pointed to two merry children

THE DOLLS.

who were laughing and chatting near, and burst into tears. At last she sobbed out : 'They're going to the great garden where the lions and tigers live, and will see lots of fine things, and I can go nowhere.'

" ' How is that, my child ?' I said.

" ' 'Cause they go to the Sunday-school, and mother won't let me go. She makes me work the whole day ; and I'm so tired of sitting here always. And I can't go to the great garden without paying a lot of money. I've been saving farthings for it a long time, but they say there isn't half enough in this,' and she handed me a dirty little bag of small coppers. 'Mother said she'd give me a holiday to-day ; but 'tisn't of any good if I can't go anywhere. I don't know when I shall get one again.'

" I felt Emily pull my dress once or twice while the poor child was speaking, and then she whispered :

" ' My bright shilling, auntie ! will grandmamma be angry ?'

" ' But, Emily dear, I thought you were going to buy a Noah's Ark with that,' I said.

" ' I can do without it, auntie,' replied Emily. ' I'd much rather *she* should have the money ; she says she never saw any fine things. Do tell her to come and fetch it : it's in my red purse at home.'

" How I wish you could have seen the poor little creature's beaming face and sparkling eyes, as Emily gave her the bright shilling an hour after our talk with her. You would not have recognized her as

the sorrowful, weeping child on the doorstep.   But
1 scarcely think she looked happier than Emily, who
skipped and jumped about the whole day, so that
one would think she had just received a shilling
instead of having given it away.   She could think
of nothing but the little girl and the great gardens.

TELLING THE STORY.

   " And now, darlings, my story is ended, and it is
quite time these little eyes were shut."

"Oh, don't leave off yet, ma!" said Clara.

"It's so interesting!" added Minnie. "Just tell us, dear ma, if the little girl enjoyed herself in the great gardens."

"Oh, yes," said Mrs. Anderson, "very much, indeed; but it would take too long now to tell you all about that; so good-night, darlings—here comes Jane;" and thanking their kind mamma for her little story, Clara and Minnie kissed her, and ran off to bed.

A little word, in kindness spoken,
  A movement, or a tear,
Has often healed the heart that's broken,
  And made a friend sincere.

## ROBIN HOOD.

THIS person is very famous in old English history and the popular ballads and traditions of the country people of England. He is supposed to have lived in the twelfth century, during the reign of Richard, surnamed Cœur de Lion.

When William duke of Normandy conquered England, and made himself king there, he introduced his Norman followers into the country, and gave them the lands of the conquered Saxons. These Norman chieftains were tyrannical and oppressive towards the country people, driving them from their farms and houses, and compelling great numbers of them to seek refuge from their oppressors in the woods and solitary places. Here they lived in bands, enjoying a sort of wild independence, and encouraging each other to keep up the old Saxon national spirit. They subsisted by hunting deer and other game ; and sometimes they attacked the Norman chiefs and plundered them. In this manner they lived in a state of outlawry, the government being unable to expel them from their hiding-places.

The most famous of these outlaws was Robin Hood. He was born at the town of Locksley, in Nottinghamshire, and dwelt in the forest of Sherwood. His favorite companions were Little John, and Friar Tuck ; the latter was said to be a monk,

ROBIN HOOD AND LITTLE JOHN.

who officiated as Robin Hood's chaplain. Robin Hood himself is often called by the old chroniclers, *Earl of Huntington,* but it is doubtful whether he had any legal claim to this title ; his true name seems to have been Robert Fitz Ooth.

His exploits were a common subject of ballads and songs from the time of Edward III., though many of these poems, now extant, appear to have been composed or altered in later times. They celebrate Robin Hood's skill in archery, and the considerate manner in which he carried on his maraudings and robberies. He was famous for robbing the rich for the purpose of giving to the poor, and this made his story a great favorite with the common people.

Stow, the old English chronicler, gives the following account of him. "In this time, about the year 1190, were many robbers and outlaws, among which Robin Hood and Little John, renowned thieves, continued in woods, despoiling and robbing the goods of the rich. They killed none but such as would invade them, or by resistance for their own defence.

"The said Robert entertained an hundred tall men, and good archers, with such spoils and thefts as he got, upon whom four hundred (were they ever so strong) durst not give the onset. He suffered no woman to be oppressed, or otherwise molested. Poor men's goods he spared, abundantly relieving them with that which, by theft, he got from abbeys, and the houses of rich earls."

Drayton, an old English poet, thus speaks of Robin Hood in his poem entitled "Polyolbion :"—

> " From wealthy abbots' chests,
>   And churches' abundant store,
> What oftentimes he took,
>   He shared among the poor.
> No lordly bishop came
>   In lusty Robin's way,
> To him before he went
>   But for his pass must pay.
> The widow in distress
>   He graciously relieved ;
> And remedied the wrongs
>   Of many a virgin grieved."

Major, the Scottish historian, declares that Robin Hood was indeed an arch robber, but " the gentlest thief that ever was." He seems to have been as famous in Scotland as in England. There is no doubt that this celebrated outlaw and his wild companions carried on their depredations without any regard to the rights of property. But it must be considered, on the other hand, that the laws and regulations established by the Norman kings of England, for the purpose of maintaining their parks and hunting grounds, were most severe and tyrannical, and directly calculated to drive the people into desperate ways of life.

William the Conqueror had no less than sixty-eight forests, thirty-one *chases*, and seven hundred and eighty-one parks, in England, for his private use. William Rufus, his successor, laid waste thirty miles of territory, by driving the country-people from their fields and dwellings, in order to form what was called *the New Forest.* By the severe "forest laws" any man who killed a deer belonging to the king, was punished by having his eyes plucked out, and other barbarous acts of mutilation.

But as the English in those days, before the discovery of gunpowder, were trained up from boyhood to the use of the long bow, and excelled all other nations of Europe in the art of shooting with this weapon, they often infringed these laws with impunity. Troops of banditti, similar to that of Robin Hood, were commonly lurking about the royal forests, and from their superior skill in archery, and their knowledge of the recesses of the wild solitudes of the country, found it no difficult matter to kill and carry off the king's deer.

How great a favorite Robin Hood was with the country people of England in former times, we may judge from the following account given by Bishop Latimer, in one of his sermons.

" I came once myself to a place, riding on a journey home from London ; and I sent word over night into the town that I would preach there in the morning because it was a holiday. And methought it was a holiday's work. The church stood in my way, and I took my horse, and my company, and went

thither. I thought I should have found a great
company in the church ; and when I came there the
church door was fast locked. I tarried there half
an hour and more ; and at last the key was found,
and one of the parish comes to me and says, 'Sir,
this is a busy day with us. We cannot hear you ;
it is Robin Hood's day. The parish are gone
abroad to gather for Robin Hood, I pray you let
[*hinder*] them not.' I was fain then to give place
to Robin Hood." The sermon in which the above
anecdote is related was preached before King Edward VI.

The exploits of this renowned outlaw have been
the theme of a great multitude of compositions
both in prose and verse ; the catalogue of the ro-
mances and ballads on this subject is very long,
and shows the general interest which the English
people of old times felt in the romantic history of
Robin Hood.

The close of Robin Hood's life has been described in the following manner. Having for a long
series of years maintained a sort of independent
sovereignty, and set kings, judges, and magistrates
at defiance, a proclamation was published offering a
considerable reward to any person who would cap-
ture him, either alive or dead. Nobody, however,
dared to attempt his arrest, or he was too much a
favorite with all his neighbors to allow them to en-
tertain any desire to see this done. At length, the

infirmities of old age came upon him, and during a
fit of sickness he found it necessary to be blooded.
For this purpose he applied to the prioress of a nun-
nery, in Yorkshire ; as the women of the religious
orders were, in that age, famous for their skill in
surgery. This woman treacherously bled him to
death, November 18, 1247, he being then in his
eighty-seventh year. He was buried under a stone
by the highway.

The following epitaph was written on him, although the language has been modernized to make
it intelligible to common readers.

> " Here underneath this little stone,
> Through Death's assaults now lieth one,
> Known by the name of Robin Hood,
> Who was a thief and archer good.
> Full thirty years and something more,
> He robbed the rich to feed the poor ;
> Therefore his grave bedew with tears,
> And offer for his soul your prayers."

HOW EDWARD SHARP GOT CURED OF HIS FAULTS.

## HOW EDWARD SHARP GOT CURED OF HIS FAULTS.

I CANNOT tell why it is, but some boys who are not very bad, do like to be in mischief. Of this kind was one of my little friends—a handsome, black-eyed fellow, by the way—named Edward Sharp.

Edward, or Ned, as we used to call him, was not ill-natured, nor ill-tempered, nor very wicked in any way ; but he dearly loved to tease people, and many a saucy joke did he play upon his youthful companions. Even his sister Jane, who was a good, kind creature as ever lived, was often made the subject of Ned's mischievous practices.

In vain did the boy's father and mother advise, caution, and threaten him for his faults and follies : a spirit of elvish fun seemed to be in his very nature. But at last he got cured in a way nobody expected.

The story is this : Ned had one day placed a pin in the bottom of a chair, with the point sticking up, and he expected somebody would sit down upon it. From this he anticipated a deal of sport. He had not put the point up very high, so as to inflict a severe wound ; but he chuckled a great deal at the idea of seeing some one bound out of the chair, as if stung by a bumble-bee.

But it chanced that no one sat down in the chair for some time, and Ned's attention being directed to something else, he forgot all about the pin. After a little time, he was caught in his own trap, for he sat down bang in the chair, and the pin entered pretty deeply into his flesh. In his agony and surprise, he jumped into the air, and uttered a terrible cry.

At first everybody in the room looked about with wonder, but pretty soon Jane went to the chair, and there seeing the pin artfully arranged, she had no difficulty in guessing at the cause of the uproar. She directed the attention of every one in the room to the pin, and at once all eyes were turned on Master Ned. He very speedily ceased crying, and hung down his head in shame. It was needless to preach a sermon to him on the occasion. He saw very clearly the moral of his adventure—which was, that *he who sets traps for others, is sure some day or other to be caught.* From that time he gave up his habit of teasing and mischief-making, and long before he was a man, he had learned to practice kindness to all around him.

## THE YELLOW ROSE.

"BOYS are very still lately after school, what makes them so ?" said Mrs. Evans, whose house stood near the Academy ; "they used to annoy us greatly by their shouts, but lately I have not heard them at all."

"Most of the larger boys have become greatly interested in gardening," said Mrs. Wilder, "hence they go home as soon as they are dismissed."

"I hope they will continue to do so. When they remain and play on the green, they make noise enough to render one distracted. I have sometimes said to Mr. Evans that we should be obliged to change our residence for one more quiet."

"Boys generally give their lungs some exercise when they leave the confinement of the schoolroom. It does them good."

"It does not do those who are condemned to hear them much good."

"It enables them to exercise the virtue of patience."

"I think if you lived here, your opinion would be different."

Mrs. Evans had no children, and hence was not quite as forbearing towards their recreations and follies as she might have been. She could not see why children need make any more noise than grown persons ; she thought they had no right to make as much. Boys are not as large as men, therefore she concluded they had no right to make as much noise as men. But she found that the facts did not agree with this logical conclusion. It was notorious that boys made more noise than men. Indeed, she seemed to think that boys were little else than noise-making machines, nuisances which ought to be

GARDENING.

abated. Of course Mrs. Evans was not remarkably popular with the boys. It is quite possible that in consequence of her peculiar opinions, **there were** louder shouts in the vicinity of **her** dwelling **than** there would otherwise have been.

But gardening **had** engaged their attention, **and Mrs.** Evans' **ears** had rest. She was sure, however, **that the** calm would not **last** long, and that when the urchins began again, they would make up the temporary deficiency with interest. Some amiable people are sure that if boys do right to-day, they will certainly do wrong to-morrow. Hence it is always proper to regard them with suspicion **and** blame.

But let **us turn our attention to the matter of** gardening. The teacher had suggested the idea to one **or two of** the leading boys, and they entered into it **with** enthusiasm. They induced their parents **to** assign them **a bit** of land **for** gardens, and **all** their leisure hours **were spent in** preparing it for flowers. Their example became contagious. All the boys rushed into gardening. Those who could not procure ground that was inclosed, appropriated portions pertaining to the highway, and inclosed them with miniature fences, which the street cows gazed at with great gravity, as they chewed the cud, and their fellow-freemen, the porkers, rooted down to see if there were any corn or potatoes within **which** they might root up.

Boys, **like** men and women, like to do what other folks do. **It** was not strange, therefore, that the cultivation of flowers was the order of the day. All the gardens in the vicinity, which contained flowers, were laid under contribution by those who were under the influence of this newly awakened zeal. The supply was limited, and the demand great. What was to be done? Flower gardens without flowers were not exactly the thing. Some thought of turning utilitarians, and of filling their gardens with corn and cabbages, but the fashion set exclusively in the direction of the ornamental, and the rebellious attempt was not made.

At length it occurred to James Halsey, that spring was nursing in the woods and fields many choice flowers which she would readily consent should be transferred to gardens, provided they were treated tenderly. Dame Nature is not willing that any of her productions should be treated unkindly and harshly. If it is done, she withdraws her countenance and support, which is sure to cause them to fade and die. If, on the other hand, men treat her offspring kindly, she will assist in rearing them, and in bringing them to a higher perfection than they would have attained in the places where they were born.

"Come," said James to Herbert Alfred, on the morning of a holiday, "let us go into the woods and find some wild flowers, and plant them in our gardens."

"I never knew any body to plant wild flowers in

the garden," said Herbert.   "Any body can see them in the woods."

"True, but it is some trouble to go to the woods to see them.   I think they will look very pretty in our gardens."

"If we could find some which nobody has seen, and were to pretend we got them from somebody's garden, a great way off, it would do, I think.   Folks would think a great deal of them, then."

"As I stock my garden to please myself, I do not care whether other folks think a great deal of my flowers or not.   I wish to get those that are really beautiful, and enjoy them."

"Well, I will go with you, but you must not let anybody know it."

"Why not?"

"Because I don't want anybody else to get any. If all the boys get them, there will be no use in having them."

Herbert was like many grown-up people.   They want many things, not because they regard them as beautiful, but because others regard them so. And they regard things as valuable in proportion as they are uncommon, and think a thing has lost all desirableness if some other person has one like it.   In their weakness and follies, boys and girls are quite as bad as men and women.

James and Herbert furnish themselves with baskets and tools, and set out for a forest which cover ed the southern side of a hill. The south wind was whispering gently to the violets, and other spring flowers, to come forth and show themselves, and, under the warm rays of the sun, they were beginning to do so. The boys soon filled their baskets with flowers and flowering shrubs, which were really more beautiful than any of the flowers and shrubs they had procured from gardens. Even Herbert, who was so much accustomed to let other persons form his opinions for him, was struck with the beauty of the violets, and said, " If these had come from England they would be prettier than anything we have."

James did not enter into controversy with him. He was content with perceiving and enjoying their beauty, which, to his eye, was as great as if they had been reared in Queen Victoria's garden. James had the rare habit of thinking for himself—of forming his own opinions.

It happened that both boys had more flowers than they had space to put them in. James perceived his surplus, and offered them to the first one that came along. He knew he would have an opportunity of disposing of them in a short time, for the boys were constantly passing round to see what progress each was making.

Herbert having set out such of his collection as he had room for, hastened to destroy the rest, before any one should come along to ask for them. He came to see James just as James was in the act of giving his surplus to **Allen Irvine, a** boy who was in feeble health, and unable to go **to the** forest himself.

"What made you such a fool **as** to give him those flowers?" said Herbert, as soon as Allen was out of hearing.

"I did not want them," said James.

"Well, why did you not throw them away?"

"Because they had good roots and will do well in his garden."

"What of that? I didn't mean to **have anybody** know we had them till it was too **late** to get any more. **Now every boy** in the place will get them, and very likely they will find handsomer ones than ours."

"That will not make ours the less beautiful."

"**If I** wanted to give them **away, I would not** have given **them to James Allen.**"

"Why not?"

"Because he is poor and sickly, and you never can get anything from him in pay."

"He seemed very thankful, and that I think is good pay."

"If you call thankfulness good pay, you can soon get rid of everything you have."

Herbert, in the conversation above **recorded,** exhibited some further traits of character which are frequently found in grown-up people. There are those who, if they have favors to bestow, will carefully confine them to those who have ability to return them. What they would call acts of benevolence are simply investments, on which they hope and expect to recover a high rate of interest. Of course, such persons know nothing of the pleasures of benevolence.

James had experience of the pleasure of benevolence when he gave his flowers to Allen. He gave them to him because he was poor and sickly, unable to get them himself, and unable to give anything in return.

Herbert's last remark seems to imply that, in his opinion, thankfulness was a commodity easily obtained. I do not agree with him. It is not often that true thankfulness, either to God or man, follows the reception of favors. I am sure Herbert would have felt very little thankfulness for any favors done him.

We must do good for its own sake, and not in order to receive benefits in return, or thankfulness from those on whom our favors are conferred.

In a certain garden, the property of a stern old man, there was a yellow rose, the only one in the village. The owner rejoiced in his sole proprietorship, and refused all applications for shoots, which it threw up abundantly from its roots.

One day, a poor ragged boy, who never attended school, and who was looked down upon and often ill treated by the school boys on account of his poverty, brought James a shoot from said rose.

" Where did you get this ?" said James, as the boy, with evident satisfaction, placed it in his hand.

" I got it at Mr. Storms'."

" How did you get it ?"

" I have been at work in his garden."

" Did he give you leave to take it ?"

" No."

" Do you suppose I want stolen goods ?"

" I didn't steal it."

" How did you get it, then ?"

" I took it."

James was half indignant and half amused at the distinction made between taking and stealing,—it is a distinction which many boys make—but it is plainly a distinction without a difference.

" I can't take it, Tom."

" Why not ?   I wanted you to have it.   I would not have taken it for any body else.   You have always treated me well."

" That is no reason why you should steal it for me."

" I didn't steal it.   Mr. Storms told me to make a bed for parsnips.   He told me to dig up every thing in it, and pick out all the roots and every thing.   In digging, I threw up this root, and I thought I might as well bring it to you as to throw it away."

This statement put a different aspect on the matter.   The idea of theft had not entered Tom's mind.

The rose was a very desirable object. Might he not without blame accept it and place it in his garden ? Many would have seen no difficulty in so doing, but James knew that there was a difference between what is *just* right and what is *not quite* right. He knew that the true standard for a man is what is just right. So, after pondering the matter for some time, he said, " I am much obliged to you for your kindness, but I will not set it out till I get Mr. Storms' permission. Do you work for Mr. Storms to-morrow ?"

" Yes."

" Well, you take this root back, and take care of it, and I will come in the morning and tell him you dug it up by mistake, and, maybe, he will let me have it."

" I know he won't."

" Perhaps he will. You take it back now to his garden."

Tom very unwillingly retraced his steps to the garden, carrying with him the rose which he supposed James would be eager to receive.

Just as he entered the garden, Mr. S., who had unexpectedly returned, met him.

" What have you there ?" said he.

" Something that I dug up in making the parsnip bed."

" What have you been doing with it ?"

" I thought it would die if it was not set out, so I took it over to James Halsey ; but he would not take it without your consent."

" Wouldn't take it ?"

" No, sir. I told him I found it among the roots you told me to dig up and throw away."

" I didn't tell you to dig up a rose-bush, you stupid ; but since there is one honest boy in the place, you may take it to him and tell him I say he may have it. But if you ever take anything out of the garden again, you will be sorry for it."

Tom did not wait to be told a second time to take the rose to its proprietor.

If the reader has paid attention to the foregoing pages, he has had several points worthy of reflection set before his mind, and has seen another illustration of the old proverb that honesty is the best policy.

## THE LOST PUZZLE.

ELL, Willie, one would think from the fuss you are making, that you had lost your best friend."

"Aunt Susan, some one has stolen my Chinese puzzle, and now I can not show it to George Lawson."

"And where did you leave it last night, when you went to bed ?"

"On the hall table, and I believe that Jim Brown, the washerwoman's boy, took it when he was here this morning."

"Be careful, Willie, how you accuse another. You may have forgotten where you laid it."

"Oh, I am certain that I left it here on this table."

"Do not be too sure. Come with me and I will see if I can not find it for you. Have you looked everywhere ?"

"Yes, high and low, in every place where I thought it likely to be. That Jim Brown has it, and I will go straight to his house, and make him give it back to me."

"Wait, and see that it is nowhere about the house."

"I know that it has gone, for I have looked everywhere."

"Not everywhere, as I have no recollection of seeing you in my room this morning, and that is the last place you had it last night."

"Every thing that I get is taken from me. All the other boys keep their toys, while mine go some way or another."

"And how do they go ?  Do you not dispose of them yourself ?  The handsome top I gave you went for a rusty knife ; your elegant glass marbles for a piece of cake.  That soon vanished, and the kite Uncle John sent, you left out in the rain, and it was of course spoiled.  Now can you tell me where they go ?"

"But this puzzle I had determined to keep, and now that Jim Brown has it."

"Hurrah !  What is this, Willie ?" said Aunt Susan, holding up the identical puzzle.

"Oh yes, I forgot I left it here last night."

"But you insisted that you left it in the hall, and knew that poor Jim Brown had it."

"As I thought it was gone, I knew that no one came in so early as Jim, so I thought he had taken it."

" Hereafter, if you lose anything never accuse any one of stealing it until you have some proof that he is really dishonest. It might affect that poor boy's character for life to be called a rogue, even by a little boy like you. Sit down by me, and I will tell you a story that will show you the evil consequences arising from accusing persons falsely.

" When I was a little girl, a lady of my mother's acquaintance came to reside here. She was very rich, and had many elegant dresses, and a great deal of costly jewelry. Among the latter was a peculiarly carved ring, with a diamond setting of great value which she always wore upon the fore finger of the left hand, and only took it off once in a great while to clean it.

" My mother, having some plain sewing to do, had engaged a young girl to come to the house and assist her. She was very poor, but honest, and strove hard to keep herself and mother comfortable, by her untiring industry. Our sewing-room was in the second story of the back building, and overlooked the garden that was beautifully laid out in stars and diamonds, decked with the richest flowers. We had a great many bees in queer-shaped hives, glassed all round, so that we might see the honey-comb formed, without disturbing the bees ; also several beautiful birds in exquisite cages, that were arranged among the flowers, giving a picturesque appearance to the view.

"One morning Mrs. Montrose—for that was the name of our visitor—was in this room, and showed this ring, which for some cause she was very proud of, to the seamstress, Julia Sawyer. In doing so, she discovered that it needed cleaning ; so she took the basin with some soap and water, and stood by the window that she might see to clean it thoroughly. She was scrubbing the ring busily, when suddenly she raised her eyes, and saw my mother's favorite canary perched upon the top of his cage. Forgetting every thing, she dropped the ring in the basin, and hastened to catch the little songster before he took refuge in the boughs of the neighboring trees. It was some time before the little prisoner was again caged. When she returned to the room, the bowl was emptied and the ring gone. In an instant, suspicion fell upon the little seamstress. In vain she protested her innocence, saying she thought Mrs. Montrose had taken it with her when she left the room. The servant who had cleaned the room during her absence was questioned closely, but knew nothing about it.

"My parents felt exceedingly annoyed to think that their friend should meet with so great a loss while a visitor at their house, and that suspicion had fallen upon one in whom they had ever reposed perfect confidence. Julia offered and insisted upon their searching her. This they would not do, because they thought she had secreted it somewhere out of the room. My father begged Mrs. Montrose not to prosecute Julia, saying that in all probability she would find it again, and, if Julia really had taken it, she might return it from fear of exposure. This kind of reasoning Mrs. Montrose would not listen to, but insisted that an example should be made of her, and if there was any justice she should go to prison.

We all felt deeply for the poor girl, who was nearly deranged. A writ was issued, and—as she had no one to go her bail (my father not being a property holder) she was carried off to jail. Her mother was apprised of her daughter's situation, and her agony, to think her darling child within the gloomy portals of the prison, is better imagined than described. She went on her knees to Mrs. Montrose, who said the law must take its course. A bill was filed against her, and at the next term of the court she was brought, pale and almost fainting, to the dock, where the most abandoned and depraved had received their sentences.

" Her mother accompanied her ; and more like shadows than human beings did they appear as they listened to the evidence which, if true, would certainly condemn her. After the testimony was taken the judge asked her if she had anything to say. Her answer was, ' I am innocent.' Of this she had no proof. She was pronounced guilty. Scarce a dry eye was in the court-room, from the judge down, with the exception of Mrs. Montrose, who thought, by punishing the poor girl, she would be repaid for her loss. The judge's voice trembled when he pronounced the sentence of two years in the State's prison, as that was the shortest time allowed for such cases. The poor agonized mother pleaded in vain to share her daughter's cell. That by law was forbidden. Henceforth, those who had lived for one another were separated, never more to meet this side the grave. Scarce a week had elapsed, ere the mother was found a cold and stiffened corpse, with the remnants of a fatal poison by her side. Julia bore with fortitude her great trials. A consciousness of innocence, and a firm reliance in One that will not forsake those who put their trust in him, bore her spirits up. But close confinement and hard work brought on disease, which ended in death, a few months after her incarceration.

"Mrs. Montrose returned home, amply repaid for her misfortune by the conviction, of the guilty, as she thought."

"Well, Aunty, I do believe Julia did take the ring, after all."

"No, my dear, she did not. Do you see the little stream that runs along through the rear of this house, in which all the sewers empty. It was some two years after the ring was lost, that two or three little boys like yourself were playing there, and selecting the pebbles for marbles, when one found, deeply embedded in the sand, the ring, the same ring. It had been thrown out in the basin of water into the sewer, and finally found its way to this little stream, where, in all probability, it would have lain until this time, had it not have been for the boys hunting pebbles. Now do you not see how wrong it is to accuse any one falsely?"

"Indeed I do, and you will not catch me doing so again. What did you do with the ring?"

"We sent it to its rightful owner, stating how and where it was found."

"I should think she must have felt very bad."

"She did grieve very much, and came on to make Julia all the reparation in her power. It was too late—she was dead. She had both mother and daughter removed to a shady nook in our cemetery, and raised a neat monument over them. Now, remember never to accuse another, without positive proof of his guilt."

## THE SLEIGH-RIDE.

ONIES, whoa! stand still there,—you will have enough to do for your little trotters before you come back. Stand still, my beauties!"

Joe Sands was more proud of his ponies than even of his own black locks and raven whiskers, which he cultivated and curled in the most approved fashion. He was now rigged out in the most magnificent style ; his ponies almost covered with strings of bells, and his beautiful scarlet cutter richly lined and cushioned, and provided with a rich fox skin robe, lined with scarlet and gold plush. His own person was enveloped in an elegant wadded wrapper, with a fine Russian beaver, from which dangled a large silken tassel.

His establishment was now drawn up before the comfortable mansion of Mr. Morris, and Joe was somewhat impatient for the appearance of the young ladies whom he was to have the honor of driving to the wedding, where he was to act as chief groomsman. With an occasional crack of the whip, and a sudden reigning in of the ponies, that made all the bells jingle again, and a loud and sharp "Whoa there !" he amused himself as well as he could, and attracted the admiring regards of a troop of idle boys, as well as some of the more grave and genteel way-farers.

"There, Aunt Judy, we *must* hurry. Those bells have shaken half a score of impatient trills, while you have been adjusting that cap of yours. One would think you expected to be the belle of the evening, and to secure the first seat in the bride's chair. Here we are, all ready—three handsome young exquisites, as we are, and waiting in all patience for one sober chaperone to finish her prinking. There, now, dear aunty, you can't improve that. You do look *so* bewitching, I don't believe Joe Sands will speak to me at all."

"Fanny—Fanny Morris, what a chatter-box you are !" replied Aunt Judy, as she turned away from the looking glass. "Did you ever think what the tongue is made for ?"

"Do hear those bells again," interrupted Fanny. "Joe is cracking his whip as if his very fingers ached with impatience, and the ponies are as restive as chained eagles. How they will fly when they once get started !"

"Dear me !" exclaimed Aunt Judy, "I am afraid of those wild ponies. I am sure they will upset us, or run away with us."

"Don't be alarmed, dear aunty," interposed the mischief-loving Susan ; "I should love dearly to be

run away with once in my life, and even an overturn
in a nice soft snow-bank would only give new spirit
to the frolic.

Aunt Judy shrugged her shoulders, put on her
last shawl, drew her boa tightly round her delicate
neck, and with a quiet " Come, girls, I am ready,"
tripped lightly down stairs.

Joe was all smiles and compliments. The ladies
were soon seated, Aunt Judy and May on the back
seat, Fanny and Susan on the front, with Joe between them. Crack went the whip, and away flew
the ponies to the music of a hundred bells. It was
a splendid afternoon. The road was as smooth as
glass. The trees were loaded with wreaths of snow
The hills, and plains, and valleys were all alike
clothed in a white mantle.

The party were in high spirits : and even Aunt
Judy laid aside her usual fears and enjoyed it highly.

" Pray, Mr. Sands," she inquired, " will the party
be large to-night ?"

" Not more than a hundred, ma'am, I think."

" A hundred, indeed ! Where will they all come
from ? and what can you do with them ?"

" They are coming from all the neighboring towns ;
from Wilton, and Turner, and Concord and Barlow,
and from twenty miles round."

Just at this moment, Frank Willis, driving his
span of black switch tails, came up behind, with his
sleigh full of girls, and made an effort to pass. Joe

Sands cracked up his ponies. Frank cracked up his blacks. Aunt Judy screamed outright ; the girls laughed and shouted, each party cheering up their driver and urging him not to be outdone by the other. On they went ; skimming the ground like swallows, up the hills and down the valleys, the ponies keeping the lead ; but the blacks, ever and anon, pressing up and stretching ahead, as if they would overreach them.

The two were thus crowding side by side, near the top of a gentle hill which overlooked the village whither they were bound. All, except Aunt Judy, were in the highest glee, shouting, laughing, and cheering their horses to their utmost speed.

On the very top of the hill, they met another sleigh, driving at an equal pace, in the opposite direction. Joe Sands, being on the right side, dashed by, with a triumphant hurra, while Frank, though he reigned up as short as he could, was soon entangled with the stranger. A moment's delay, and a word of advice from the stranger, and Frank was pushing on again with redoubled speed.

The descent was long and irregular. About half way down, where there was a slight curve in the road, it was traversed by a little brook, which being choked with snow and ice, had overflowed the bridge, and spread a sheet of ice along the way for several yards. To Joe, who knew nothing of this, a catastrophe was inevitable. The sleigh slewed round sharply against the frozen track and capsized, with all its precious cargo, into a deep drift on the roadside.

"Oh, me ! I am killed," screamed Aunt Judy, "and all the girls with me !"

"It will take the starch out of **that** beautiful cap, **aunty** dear," said the mischievous Susan, **who** chanced **to** be at the top of the heap.

"Whoa, ponies !" **screamed** Joe Sands, as he lifted himself from **under the** double burden of that fox skin robe, which had well nigh smothered him, and Fanny and Susan who, being well wrapped up in it, had fallen with it. "Whoa, ponies !"

But the ponies were half a mile down the **road** with the sleigh in good order behind them, and Frank Willis, who had been cautioned against this danger, was just dashing **by,** vainly **endeavoring to rein up** his blacks **for** the rescue. But they took a sudden offence **at the** apparition **of Joe Sands** starting up from under the fox skin robe, and became entirely unmanageable. They reared and plunged, and then sprang away with the speed of the wind, giving no heed to the bit, nor to the soothing voice of their master.

"Whoa, ponies," shouted Joe again, trying **to** brush the mist from his **eyes.**

"Dear aunty, are you hurt ?" asked **Mary, as** soon as she came to her feet.

"Not hurt, but killed," groaned the good lady, shaking the snow from her shawl.

"Oh, that immaculate cap, dear aunty," said Susan, archly.

"Is this the way to Barlow?" asked the bewildered lady. "So much for your wild, giddy pranks. Where are we? Are you all alive?"

"Never more so," replied Fanny; "but in no plight for a dance."

"Where are those ponies?" screamed Joe, now just restored to his senses.

"There they go," replied Fanny; "just dashing round the old church yonder."

The distance to the place of rendezvous was yet some four or five miles. What should they do? Aunt Judy looked grave and uneasy; but, fortunately for Joe, she did not speak. Joe had all the sputtering to himself, and he laid it out freely upon the road, the ponies, and Frank Willis, who, he said, "was always in his way." Fanny and Susan enjoyed the accident highly, and exerted all their powers of mirth and wit to turn a seeming disaster into a frolic.

When Joe Sands had completely recovered his self-possession, he entered into the frolic with a good grace, and proposed that the ladies should seat themselves upon the buffalo, in a snug little nook by the roadside, wrapped in the fox skin robe, while he ran on to search for the run away ponies. He also insisted upon leaving his own beautiful wrapper, as an additional security to Aunt Judy against the cold.

Sands had been gone about an hour, and the little party were getting exceedingly merry, when Elder Staples, from the Shaker village, passed down the road, driving the great market sleigh of the society, on his way to Boston.

Attracted by a sudden outburst of laughter from the girls, which he naturally enough, mistook for a scream, Elder Stephen drew up by the roadside, alighted from his comfortable seat, and began to search for the cause. The jingling of his bells had put the noisy girls upon their guard, and all their mirth ceased in a moment. Without any further noise to guide him, the benevolent Shaker followed the foot tracks, and soon came upon their retreat.

It was a singular meeting. Aunt Judy arose, with dignity, and explained their accident, and the object of their waiting ; while the girls found new cause for merriment in this discovery.

" Won't thee take a seat in my sleigh ?" said Broadbrim. " I am going thy way, and have room for all." Thank you, friend," replied Aunt Judy, " we are expecting Mr. Sands every moment."

" But, may be he will not overtake his horses as soon as he expected. May be the sleigh will be broken, and I fear thee will catch cold here. If friend Joseph should be coming after thee, we shall meet him on the way."

" Elder Stephen's arguments appeared sound and reasonable ; and all the ladies were soon seated, wrapped in the blankets and covered all over with the fine robes of Mr. Sands' sleigh.

It was a quiet ride that followed. Friend Stephen's horses were as fat and sleek as himself, and moved on with an even pace, though a slow one. The very bells seemed to gingle a grave and quiet music, and all the party partook of the same spirit. Not a word was spoken for the first half hour.

"What house would thee like to stop at?" at length asked Stephen.

"At the sign of the Bell, if you please," replied Aunt Judy.

A few moments after they stopped at the sign of the Bell. Stephen received the thanks of the party with a benevolent smile, and "a thee is all welcome," and drove his way.

"Dear me!" exclaimed Mary, as she stepped in upon the floor of the tavern, "where is my slipper! I do believe I must have left it in the Shaker's sleigh."

At that moment Frank Willis came up from a cross-road, into which he had driven his frightened horses to cool them down.

"Have you seen the ponies?" cried Fanny.

"Is Joe's beautiful sleigh safe?" asked Susan.

"Where is Mr. Sands?" inquired Aunt Judy.

"Where is my slipper?" cried Mary—all in the same moment.

Willis had seen nothing of Sands or his ponies.

He was not a little vexed that the old Shaker had deprived him of the honor and pleasure of picking up the shipwrecked ladies. They were all now thrown into additional trouble about Joe, and gathering around the cheerful fire, they considered what should be done.

Meanwhile, the crest-fallen Joe had accepted the proffered aid of a kind farmer, who, in coming down the road on horseback, attempted to arrest the mad flight of the ponies ; but, in doing so, only caused them to dash off into another road, which led them back toward home.

Joe mounted on behind the farmer, and off they went, as fast as Dobbin could go under his double burden. The ponies were at length brought up at a turnpike-gate, some seven or eight miles from the place of their starting. There Joe came up with them, but he was obliged to pause awhile, to give them breath. When all was ready, he drove with all speed to the scene of his late disaster.

To his utter consternation, the ladies were gone. Where could they be ? Which way had they gone ? Had they walked on to the place of meeting, or had they gone back toward home ? Joe was in a sad quandary ; but the last question that came up seemed to turn the scale of his doubts. He con-cluded that Aunt Judy was sick with her exposure, and that they had all gone on their way home.

Without stopping to consider how they could get

along with the burden of the buffalo and sleigh robe, he cracked his whip, and drove briskly on toward home. Poor Joe! the evening was cold, he had neither wrapper nor buffalo, and he was going the wrong way.

The company at the Bell Tavern was increasing. Several other parties bound to the same festival, had dropped in. Among them was an eccentric, humorous, impulsive naval officer, of about five and twenty, who, on his way down, had fallen in with Elder Stephen, at the neighboring village. The honest Shaker, finding he was to stop at the "Sign of the Bell," requested him to take charge of a little shoe, which he had just found among the blankets in his sleigh. "It must belong," said he, "to one of the little women I picked up on the way, and left at the Bell."

"A real Cinderella!" exclaimed the Captain; "and I'll find her, though they hide her under the most obscure wash-tub in the country."

The Elder wondered what he meant, but said nothing. Quietly resuming his seat, he drove on towards the city, while the enthusiastic young officer sprang into his sleigh, and dashed down the road in eager anticipation of a new adventure.

When Captain Armstrong arrived at the Bell, he was ushered into the common parlor, where a large party was already assembled, preparing to start for the nuptial festival. Mary Morris was in a sad dilemma, since she was to act as chief bridesmaid, which she could hardly do, becomingly, with **one** unslippered **foot.** It was arranged with her sisters that she **should share** with them, by turns, so that, in presenting herself before the altar, with the bride, she should be fully equipped. She was just arranging **a** beautiful Indian moccasin upon the unfortunate **foot, as the** door opened, and the gallant captain, with a flushed countenance and a profusion of bows, presented himself before them, exclaiming, " Cinderella ! Cinderella ! where art thou, beautiful, injured maiden ?"

The whole company were equally amazed **and** amused by this singular apostrophe. All conversation ceased in an instant ; the half-adjusted shawl was **left hanging** carelessly over **the arm ; the** half-tied **hat** fell back **upon the chair ; the half-turned curls** hung **in** dishevelled luxuriousness **upon** the blushing cheek, and that beautiful moccasin, scarcely drawn over the delicate foot of Cinderella, still left the heel and ankle exposed. All eyes were turned upon the captain. Not at all abashed by being the object of such curiosity, the bold and self-possessed cavalier advanced to the midst of the circle, and looking earnestly at every group, and every individual, reiterated his eager call for Cinderella. " Come forth !" he said, " wherever thou **art, under** whatever tub thy envious sisters have concealed thee, come forth !"

Peering carefully round, Mary's half-dressed foot, projecting from under the ample folds of her pelisse, caught his eye.    He was instantly at her feet, and before she had recovered her self-possession suffi- ciently to withdraw the exposed foot, he had seized the moccasin, pulled it off, and adjusted the lost slip- per in its place.

"A fit—a perfect fit!" he exclaimed.    "Cinder- ella! most lovely, most fortunate! all the fairies be- friend thee, and——"

A general burst of laughter from the whole com- pany, followed by a furious blast of the tavern horn as a signal that it was time to be moving, inter- rupted the gallant captain in his rhapsody, and left the blushing Mary to finish her preparations for the fete.

The nuptial party was large, yet very select.    The bride was beautiful ; the bridegroom splendid ; the house was brilliantly illuminated, and all things were ready.    But where was Joe Sands, the chief groomsman ?

The minister had come, the bridegroom had taken the bride's hand to lead her forward ; and Captain Armstrong, by appointment, was about to supply Joe's place in the ceremony, with Mary Morris, the Cinderella of the evening, leaning on his arm, when the door flew open, and Sands, the veritable Joe Sands, sprang in.

It was a sad disappointment to the captain, but

he gracefully yielded the blushing Mary to his rival, and the ceremony went on.

When the knot was tied, and while the good minister **was** greeting the fair bride with a paternal kiss, Joe **began** to **enquire** of Mary **by what** means they **reached** the village. **The story of the** overturn, **the good old** Shaker, **and the lost** slipper, afforded **no little** mirth, and made Cinderella **the belle of the** evening.

**But** Judge Weston, a kind-hearted, fine-looking widower from Barlow, to the utter neglect of the young girls, was taken with such a sympathy for their quiet Aunt Judy, and **so** much moved with fear lest she should meet a similar accident on the way home, that he insisted upon taking her into his **own carriage**; "for I **have a** very careful **driver**," said he, "**and I** will see you safely to your **own** door."

Aunt Judy accepted the **offer.** The evening was unusually brilliant. The ride was agreeable to all parties. Sands and Willis raced back without accident or adventure. Captain Armstrong looked after them longingly, but was obliged to go the other way. What passed in the Judge's carriage was shrewdly conjectured, but never fully known. **Be**fore the snow was gone, the worthy man **had passed** that way often, and never without calling at Mr. Morris'; and **ere** the spring had put forth her blossoms, our beloved aunt had changed her name

to Weston, and gone down to Barlow, to clear away
from the Judge's house the frost work of a five
years' widowhood, by shedding over it again the
sunshine of home.

---

## AN ADVENTURE.

T O celebrate his daughter's wedding,
a merchant collected a party of her
young companions.  They circled
around her ; wishing much happiness to the
youthful bride and her chosen one.   Her
father gazed proudly on his lovely child, and hoped
that as bright prospects for the future might open
for the rest of his children, who were playing among
the guests.   Passing through the hall of the base-
ment, he met a servant who was carrying a lighted
candle in her hand, without a candlestick.  He
blamed her for such conduct, and went into the
kitchen to see about supper.  The girl soon returned, but without the candle.  The merchant

immediately recollected that several barrels of gunpowder had been placed in the cellar during the day, and that one had been opened.

" Where is your candle ?" he enquired in the utmost alarm.

"I couldn't bring it up with me, for my hands are full of wood," said the girl.

" Where did you put it ?"

" Well, I had no candlestick, so I stuck it in some black sand that's in the small barrels."

Her master went down stairs. The passage was long and dark, his knees threatened to give way under him, his breath was choked, his flesh seemed dry and parched, as if he clearly felt the suffocating blast of death. At the end of the cellar, under the room where his children and their friends were reveling in felicity, he saw the open barrel of powder full to the top, the candlestick loosely in the grains with a long red snuff or burnt wick. The sight seemed to wither all his powers. The laughter of the company struck upon his ear like the knell of death. He stood a moment unable to move. To the music above, the feet of the dancers responded with vivacity, the floor shook, and the loose bottles in the cellar jingled with the motion. He fancied the candle moved—was falling. With desperate energy he sprang forward. But how to remove it—the slightest touch would cause the red hot wick to fall into the powder. With unequalled presence of mind he placed a hand on each side of the candle, with the open palm upwards, and the fingers pointed towards the object of his care, which, as his hands met, was secured in the claspings of his fingers, and safely moved away from its dangerous position.

When he reached the head of the stairs, he smiled at his previous alarm, but the reaction was too powerful, and he fell into fits of the most violent laughter.    He was conveyed to his bed senseless, and many weeks elapsed ere his nerves recovered sufficient tone to allow him to resume his business.

## THE THREE WISHES.

"AH !" said George, "if I might choose, I'd rather be Julius Cæsar than any other man that lived ! He was a fine fellow, he conquered all the then known world—from the pyramids of Egypt to the island of Thule—from the most remote provinces of Asia Minor to the western shores of the Peninsula. In ten years only, he took eight hundred cities, subdued three hundred nations, and left above a million of enemies dead upon his fields of battle ! Now he *was* a hero ! And what a glorious thing it must have been, after subduing Britons, Gauls, Germans, and Russians, to return with his triumphant legions, laden with spoil, and leading kings captive, a conqueror in the streets of Rome ! I never think of Julius Cæsar without longing to be a soldier. 'He came—he saw—he conquered !' How famous that was ! I wish I had lived in his days ; or, better still, I wish there was another world to conquer, and I was the Julius Cæsar to do it."

"Upon my word !" said Charles, "mighty grand !

but if I might choose, I would rather be Cicero. I'd rather be an orator ten thousand times than a warrior, though he were Julius Cæsar himself. Only think, George, when you come to die, how should you like to have the blood of a million of men on your conscience? Depend upon it, it's not such a fine thing to be a conqueror, after all! But an orator! his *is* a glorious character indeed. He gains

victories over millions, without shedding one drop of blood! Now let us match ourselves one against the other; you a warrior, I an orator—each, let us

suppose, the most accomplished in the world.  What
can you do without your legions and your arms ?
With ten thousand men at your back, armed at all
points, where, pray, is the wonder that you take
possession of a city or a country, weakly defended
perhaps, both by men and means ?  But place me
among savages, (provided only I can speak their
tongue) give me no arms—no money ; nay, even
strip me of my clothes, and leave me a defenceless,
solitary being among thousands, and what will follow ?—I will draw tears from the strongest heart
among them ;—they shall give me bread to eat,
clothing to wear,—they shall build a house to cover
me,—and, if my ambition extends so far, they shall
choose me for their king ; and this only by the
words of my mouth.  Now who, I ask you, is most
powerful, you or I ?

"You think it was a glorious thing for Julius
Cæsar to pass with his captives through the streets
of Rome.  I think it was glorious, too, for Cicero,
when, after having exposed and defeated the horrible conspiracy of Cataline, and driven him from
Rome, he was borne by the most honorable men of
the city to his house, along streets crowded with
thousands of inhabitants, all hailing him ' Father
and savior of his country !'  I wish I could be a
Cicero, and you might be a Julius Cæsar and an
Alexander the Great for me.

"But come, William," said he, addressing his

other brother,—"who would you choose to be ?—
and what argument can you bring forward in favor
of your choice ?"

"I," replied William, "would choose to be John
Smeaton."

"John Smeaton," questioned Charles ; "and
pray, who in the world was John Smeaton ?"

"Bless me," said George, "not know John
Smeaton ! He was a cobbler, to be sure, and wrote
a penny pamphlet, to prove how superior wooden
shoes are to Grecian sandals !"

"Not he, indeed !" interrupted William, indig-
nantly ; "he built the Eddystone Lighthouse !'

"O, yes—yes—to be sure he did ! I wonder
I should forget it," replied George. "He was a
stone-mason, and had the honor of building a wall !
—Upon my word, sir, yours is a noble ambition !
Why, Smeaton only did what any man might do !"

"Not so, either, my good Julius Cæsar !" said
William. "There are not ten men in England
that could have built that lighthouse as well as
Smeaton did. It will stand while the world stands.
It is a noble proof of the power and ingenuity of
man. It defies the almost omnipotent ocean itself,
and the other elements can never affect it.

"And now, George, consider Smeaton's case without your soldierly prejudices. Independently of his
work being a masterpiece of human skill, its importance will not be lessened by time. Your conquests,

most potent Cæsar! are wrested from you in your life-time, and your successor will hardly thank you for exhausting your country's treasure, and reducing its population, for a distant empire, which, as soon as you have left it, rises in insurrection, and almost needs re-conquering. Every year, on the contrary, makes that work of Smeaton additionally valuable; and as the commerce of the country increases, the importance of that wall, as you are pleased to term it, increases also. There's not a ship that comes into the sea but owes its preservation, in a great measure, to that light-house. Thousands of lives are preserved by it; and, when I think of it on a tempestuous night, as I often do, shining out like a star, when every other star is hidden, a blessing springs into my heart on the skill of that man who, when the endeavor seemed hopeless, confidently went to work and succeeded.

" But I'll tell you a story now, about neither Julius Cæsar, Cicero, nor John Smeaton, and yet which is quite *apropos*.

" There was, once upon a time, a little city that stood by the sea. It was very famous—it had abundance of treasure—twenty thousand soldiers to defend its walls—and orators the most eloquent in the world. You may be sure it could not exist without enemies; its wealth created many, and its pride provoked more. Accordingly, by some Julius Cæsar of those days it was besieged. Twelve thou-

sand men encamped round its walls, which extended
on three sides, and a powerful fleet blockaded the
fourth, which lay open to the sea. The inhabitants
of this little city felt themselves of course, amazing-
ly insulted by such an attack, and determined immediately to drive their audacious enemies like chaff
before the wind. They accordingly sallied out, but,
unfortunately, were driven back, and were obliged to
shelter themselves behind their walls. Seven times
this occurred, and the enemy had now been seven
months encamped there : it was a thing not to be
borne, and a council was called in the city.

"'Fight! fight!' cried the orators ; 'fight for
your homes—for the graves of your fathers—for the
temples of your gods!' But in seven defeats the
soldiers had been reduced to ten thousand, and the
people were less enthusiastic about fighting than the
orators expected. Just then a poor man came forward, and stepping upon the rostrum begged to propose three things ;—first, a plan by which the enemy might be annoyed ! second, a means of supply-
ing the city with fresh water, of which it began to
be much in need ; third—but scarcely had he named
a third, when the impatient orators bade him hold
his peace, and the soldiers thrust him out of the as-
sembly, as a cowardly proser, who thought the city
could be assisted any way, except by the use of arms.
The people seeing him so thrust forth, directly concluded that he had proposed some dishonorable

means—perhaps had been convicted of a design to betray the city ; they therefore joined the outcry of the soldiers, and pursued him with many insults to his humble dwelling, which they were ready to burn over his head.

"Now this poor man, who had never in all his life wielded a sword, and who had no ambition to do so, and who was but an indifferent speaker, was nevertheless a wise mathematician, and had wonderful skill in every mechanical science then known, which he had the ability, as is common with such men, to apply admirably to every emergency. But he might as well have had no science at all, for any respect it won him ; and though he was a little chagrined that his well-meant proposition had met no better reception, he shut to his doors, sat down in his house, and turned over his schemes in his head, till he was more sure than ever of their success. In the meantime the enemy brought up monstrous battering-rams, crow-feet, balistæ, and all kinds of dreadful engines for the demolishing of the walls, setting fire to the houses, and otherwise distressing the inhabitants. A thousand men were despatched to cut down a neighboring forest, from the trees of which they began to build immense wooden towers, whence they could sling masses of rock into the city. There was a deafening noise all day and all night without the walls, of deadly preparation. The distress of the besieged was now intolerable, and a truce was eagerly desired. A deputation, therefore, of the most honorable citizens, headed by the most eloquent orators, and preceded by a herald bearing a white flag, went to the camp of the enemy. The orators addressed them in the most powerful, and, as they thought, most soul-touching words; they craved only a truce of seven days; but their words fell like snow-flakes upon a rock; they moved no heart to pity, and the orators were sent back to their city with many marks of ignominy. 'Go back,' said they, 'and our answer shall reach the city before you do.' Accordingly every machine was put in motion. Arrows, hurled by the balistæ, fell into the streets like hail, and ponderous stones, falling upon the buildings, threatened destruction to all. The rest of that day the inhabitants kept within their houses, for there was no security in the streets, nor, it must be confessed, much within doors. The next day, when the enemy a little relaxed their efforts, the people ventured out, but nothing was heard save lamentations and murmurs.

" 'We have no bread,' said the people; 'we are dying of thirst; the little corn that remains, and a few skeleton cattle are reserved for the soldiers, while we are perishing in the streets! We will open the gates to the enemy rather than see our children die thus before our eyes!'

" Upon this the orators again came forth. It was now no use mounting the rostrum, the people were sullen, and would not assemble to hear them ; they therefore came into the streets, and poured forth their patriotic harangues to the murmuring thousands that stood doggedly together. 'Will ye,' they exclaimed, 'give up the city of your fathers' glory to their bitterest enemies ? Speak ! —will ye, can ye do it ?' And the people held up their pale and famishing children, saying, 'These are our answer—these shall speak for us !'

"Just at that moment, the poor man, filled with compassion for his townspeople and suffering from want equal to their own, stepped forward. 'Fellow-townspeople,' said he, 'listen ! There is no need for us and our children to die of hunger ;—there is no need for us to deliver up the city. Only do as I say, and we shall have plenty of provision, and may drive our enemies to the four winds.'

" ' What would you have us do ?' asked the people.

" ' Why,' said he, 'for every engine that the enemy brings, bring out one also : defy their battering-rams—disable their crow-feet—sink a shaft to the river, and have water in plenty ! Give me but seven days, three brave men, and the means I shall ask, and I will pass through the enemy's fleet, visit the cities which are friendly to us, and return with provisions to stand out the siege yet ten months longer.'

"Try him ! try him !' said they ; 'we cannot be worse than we are.'

" There was an instant re-action in favor of the
poor man ; all fell to work at his bidding ;—every
smith's shop rang with the sound of hammers ;—
carpenters worked all day and all night construct-
ing machines which were enigmas to them. There
was such a hum of business for two whole days, that
the enemy could not imagine what was going forward. In a short time all was ready. A huge machine, the height of the walls, was raised, furnished
with a tremendous pair of iron shears ; and no sooner
had the enormous crow-foot of the enemy reared
itself to pull down a part of the wall, than the
shears, catching hold of it, snapped it in two.

" A roar of applause echoed through the city, and
this first successful effort assured them all. The
poor man at once obtained the confidence of the
city ; all the enemy's deadly machines he counter-
acted ; he set fire to their immense wooden tower
by balls of inflammable matter, which he flung in
at night ; and these exploding suddenly, with horrible cracking and hissings, terrified the enemy almost out of their senses, and bursting up into vol-
cano-like fires, threatened to consume not only the
tower but the very camp itself. While this was
doing the poor man and his three colleagues passed
through the fleet in the twilight, in a small vessel
constructed for the purpose, which floating on the
surface of the water, looked only like a buoy loosen-
ed from its hold. No sooner were they outside the

fleet than they cut away one of the enemy's large
boats that lay moored on the shore ; and, hoisting
full sail, by help of a favorable wind and good rowing, they arrived by the end of the next day at a
friendly city.   There they soon obtained supplies,—
corn, salted meat, fresh-killed cattle, and everything
of which they stood in need.   A large vessel was
immediately stored and properly manned ; her hull
was blackened, so were her masts and sails, and by
good rowing, she reached the outside of the harbor
by the next evening.   There they waited till it was
quite dark, and then with every oar muffled, silently as the fall of night, yet swiftly as a bird, they
passed through the midst of the fleet without being
detected ; and by the next daybreak the vessel lay
moored upon the quay of the city.

"That, indeed, was a morning of triumph !   Men,
women, and children, thronged down in thousands.
Food was abundant ; they all ate and were satisfied.
But the extent of the poor man's service was not
known when they merely satisfied their hunger ;—
he had induced the friendly city to send yet further
supplies, with a fleet which should not only attack
the enemy's ships, but land a body of soldiers whose
object would be to fall suddenly upon the camp in
the rear, while the soldiers in the city made a sally
on the front.   Accordingly, the next day, the sea
outside the harbor was covered with ships.   The enemy was in great consternation.   All fell out as the

poor man had foreseen. After very little fighting, the enemy had permission to retire, leaving as hostages three of their principal men, till an amount of treasure was sent in which quite made up the losses of the siege.

"As you may suppose, after this, nobody thought they could sufficiently honor the poor man; his deeds were written in the annals of the city, and ever after he was universally called 'the savior of his country.'

"And so you see, the poor man, by his science and skill, could do more for his city than either soldiers or orators."

"Upon my word," said both the brothers in the same breath, "there's truth in it."

# THE COURTSHIP OF THE STORK-CALIF.

## CHAPTER I.

T was on one fine summer's evening, Chasid, the calif of Bagdad, was lazily reclining upon his sofa. After having slept awhile, for it was exceedingly warm, the calif awoke in a very good humor. He was smoking from a long rosewood pipe, drinking, at intervals, the fragrant coffee which a slave held for him ; and while tasting it, he stroked, with an air of great satisfaction, his long, fine beard. In short, any one could see at a glance that the calif was in a happy frame of mind.

At such times, his highness appeared very affable, and exhibited much condescension and kindness even to the lowest of his subjects who brought any business to him. Therefore this was the hour that Manzour, his grand vizier, had selected to pay his daily visit to him. The grand vizier came this day as usual to the palace ; but, what was very unusual with him, his countenance wore a very serious aspect.

"Ah, why do you have such a sober countenance, grand vizier?" said the surprised calif, taking for an instant his pipe from his lips.

"My lord," replied the vizier, crossing his arms upon his breast, and bowing very low, "I was not conscious that my countenance betrayed, in spite of myself, the secret thoughts of my heart; but I just now saw, as I entered here, a Jew who was displaying such fine merchandize, that I confess to you that I was much vexed that I had not more money."

The calif, who had sought for a long time for some opportunity of bestowing a favor upon his grand vizier, for whom he had a real affection, made a sign to one of his slaves to go and bring the merchant.

The Jew came as soon as he was commanded. He was a little man, with a dusky skin, and a nose shriveled and crooked, his upper lip thin, and turned upon either side by two large yellow teeth, the only ones that remained in his mouth. His little green, serpent-looking eyes glittered like fire under his heavy eyebrows. As soon as he appeared before the calif, he touched the floor with his forehead, and advanced as if he were crawling, while, with the appearance of smiling, he displayed the most frightful grin that ever spread itself upon a human countenance. He carried before him, suspended by a large strap which hung from his crooked shoulders, a box of sandal-wood, in which were packed all kinds of precious wares, which his black, hairy hand displayed to the eyes of his customers with the skill-ful cunning of a true son of Judea.

There were pearls of Ophir, hung in ear-rings, gold rings, studded with diamonds, which the eye could scarcely look at, so great was their brilliancy; also richly wrought pistols, onyx stones, ivory combs, inlaid with gold, and a thousand other jewels not less rare and costly. After having examined them all, the calif bought for Manzour, and for himself, magnificent pistols, and for the wife of his vizier, a wrought silver comb, surrounded with a crown of fine pearls, which made it the richest and the most beautiful thing in the world.

As the merchant was about closing his box, the calif, who could not take his eyes off from it, dis-covered a little drawer which had not been opened, and asked if he had not some other jewels there. The merchant opened the little apartment which the calif pointed out, and took from it a kind of snuff-box, containing a black powder wrapped in a paper, written over with singular characters, of which neither Chasid nor Manzour could decipher a single word.

"This box came to me," said the Jew, "from a merchant who had found it in the road going to Mecca. I do not know what it is; however, it is at your service, if you wish for it. I know nothing at all about it."

The calif, although very ignorant, gladly collected in the shelves of his library all kinds of curiosities and old parchments. He bought the snuff-box and the manuscript, and dismissed the merchant, who walked out backward, bowing as low as when he entered.

Chasid contemplated joyfully his acquisition ; but not, however, without earnestly wishing that he knew what was signified by the writing on the paper, which he turned over mechanically in his hands.

" Do you not know any person who can read to me this writing ?" said he, at last, to his grand vizier.

" Most gracious lord," replied the latter, " I know a man, just opposite the grand mosque, who is called Selim the Learned. He understands, they say, all languages. Send some one to seek him ; perhaps he can explain these mysterious characters."

Two slaves were sent to find Selim the Learned, with orders to bring him there immediately.

" Selim," said the calif to him as he entered, " I am told that you are versed in the knowledge of all languages. Examine this writing, and see if you can read it. If you can explain it to me, I will give you a holiday dress entirely new ; but if you are unable to read it, you shall be beaten with twelve blows and twenty-five strokes upon the soles of your feet, for having usurped the noble name of " The Learned."

Selim bowed, and replied, "Let your will be done, master." Then he considered attentively the writing which had been given him. Suddenly he exclaimed, "It is Latin, my lord, or may I be hanged !"

"Well, Latin or Greek, tell us quickly what is there," said the calif, impatiently.

Selim hastened to translate it, and read thus : "Whoever thou art who findest this article, thank Allah for the favor he has deigned to give thee. He who takes a pinch of the powder contained in this box, and says at the same time, MUTABOR (I will be changed,) the same shall be changed, according to his own desire, into whatever animal he pleases, and shall also understand the ideas which those animals communicate in their language. If he shall wish again to return to the human form, let him bow three times towards the East while pronouncing the same word, and the charm is broken. Only beware, oh, thou who attemptest this ordeal— beware of *laughing* while thou art changed !— Otherwise the magic word will irrecoverably escape from thy memory, and thou wilt be condemned to remain forever in the race of animals."

As soon as Selim had finished the translation of the cabalistic paper, the calif experienced such a degree of pleasure, that he could hardly contain himself. After having made the wise man swear never to reveal to any person the secret which he possessed, he hastened to send him away, but not before he had clothed him with a magnificent robe of silk, which added not a little to the respect which Selim the Learned already enjoyed in Bagdad.

He had hardly departed when the calif gave himself up to his joy. "This is what I call a famous bargain," exclaimed he. "What pleasure, my dear Manzour, to be able to be changed into an animal! To-morrow morning, you come and find me; we will go together into the fields; we will take my precious snuff-box, and then we shall understand all that is spoken and sung, whispered and murmured, in the air and in the water, in the woods and in the fields."

## CHAPTER II.

THE night seemed very long to the impatient calif. At length the morning dawned, and immediately, to the great surprise of his slaves, Chasid rose from his bed. He had scarcely taken his breakfast and dressed, when his grand vizier presented himself, as he had been commanded, to accompany him in his walk.

Without any delay, the calif slipped into his girdle the magic snuff-box; and, taking the arm of his vizier, after having commanded his attendants to wait behind, he commenced immediately, in company with his faithful Manzour, this venturesome expedition.

They walked through the large gardens of the palace, but in vain ; they did not meet a single thing upon which to try their magic skill. At last, the grand vizier proposed to go farther, to a pond, where he had often seen, he said, many animals of

various kinds, and especially some storks, whose awkward gait and singular chuckings had always arrested his attention. The calif gladly agreed to the proposal of his vizier, and they both proceeded towards the indicated way. Just as they reached the borders of the pond, our two friends perceived an old stork walking slowly, to and fro, hunting for frogs, and muttering, I know not what, with his long beak ; and at the same time they noticed in the air, at a great height, another of these birds, whose flight appeared to be directed toward that side.

" I will wager my beard, gracious lord," said the vizier, " that these two birds are going to converse with each other. What say you ? Shall we change ourselves into storks ?"

" With all my heart," replied the calif; " but first let us recall the way by which we can become men again."

" Nothing is easier," said the vizier, in a bold voice ; " we must bow thrice toward the East while saying ' MUTABOR.' "

" And I shall become the calif, and you the vizier," interrupted the calif. " But we must not laugh ; for if we do, we are certainly lost."

While the calif was speaking, they distinctly perceived, soaring above their heads, and gradually descending toward the earth, the stork, which at first seemed only a black spot in the sky. Unable to wait longer, he quickly drew the snuff-box from his girdle ; he took from it a large pinch—then, presenting it to his vizier, who did the same, they both exclaimed, " MUTABOR !"

The magic word was scarcely spoken, when their

legs shriveled up and became slim and brown.　At
the same instant, the beautiful yellow slippers of
the calif, and those of his companion, turned into
the ugly feet of a stork ; their arms became wings,
their necks shot out an ell above their shoulders ;
and, finally, to complete the change, their beards
vanished, and their bodies were covered with soft
hair.

"You have a very fine beak, sir," cried the calif,
arousing from his great surprise.　"By the beard of
the Prophet ! I have never seen any thing equal to
this."

"I thank you very respectfully," replied the grand
vizier, bending his long neck ; "but if I may be
allowed, I would say to your highness that, for my
part, it seems to have a rather better appearance in
a stork than in a calif."

"Flatterer," said the calif, "the metamorphosis
has not changed you."

"No, indeed," declared the vizier, with the greatest seriousness, "I have told you only the truth.
But come a little, if you please, toward the side of
our comrades, and let us see if we know truly how
to speak like a stork."

While they had been thus conversing, the stork
had reached the ground.　After having carefully
cleaned her feet, and arranged her feathers by means
of her beak, she advanced towards the hunter of
frogs, who was continuing still the same employ-

ment. The calif and his vizier hastened to join them—and I leave you to imagine what was their astonishment on hearing the following dialogue :

"Good-morning, Madam Longshanks—if, indeed, it is morning upon the earth."

"A thousand thanks, my dear Miss Pretty Bill. I was just going to fish for a little breakfast, which I shall be very much honored if you will take with me. A quarter of a lizard, or a leg of a frog, will, perhaps, agree with you."

"I am much obliged ; but I have no appetite : I have come to this field for another purpose. I am to dance this evening at a great ball which my father gives, and I wish to practice a little by myself."

Saying thus, the young stork began to leap about and to describe upon the field the most grotesque figures. The calif and the grand vizier gazed upon everything with staring eyes and wide-open beaks, hardly able to repress their astonishment. But when the young dancer, in the last figure, stood upon one foot in the position of a sylph, bending her body, and flapping gracefully her wings, they could not restrain themselves any longer. A loud laugh burst from them, so powerful and so irresistible, that it was some time before they could control it.

The calif spoke first. "Truly," exclaimed he, "this is a good jest, a fine amusement. It is only

too bad that those foolish birds were frightened at
our laughter ; had it not been for that, they were
just going to sing."

Just then the vizier remembered that laughing
was strictly forbidden during their metamorphosis,
under the penalty of forever remaining a beast, and
this thought hushed his gayety ; his countenance
became pale ; he imparted to the calif his trouble.

" I declare," exclaimed the calif, " by Mecca and
Medina ! this will be a very bad joke if I have got
to be a stork. But stop ; let us think a little what
we must do to change ourselves. I have not the
least idea."

" We must bow thrice toward the east," replied
the vizier, quickly ; " saying at the same time, Mu
—Mu—Mu—what is the word ? But let us try—
perhaps it will come to us."

So the two storks saluted the sun, and bowed so
low that their long beaks grazed the earth. But
oh, miserable ones ! the magic word had fled from
their memory. In vain the calif bowed and bowed
again ; in vain Manzour exhausted himself in crying
Mu—Mu—Mu. They had both of them lost the
remembrance of the last syllables.

And now, indeed, the unhappy Chasid and his
unfortunate vizier were changed into storks, and
remained in a feathered condition much longer than
they had wished.

## CHAPTER III.

OUR two poor unfortunate beings wandered slowly about the fields, their brain wearied with the endeavors they had made to break the charm which held them captives, and in their misery they knew not what to do. For an instant they bethought themselves of returning to the city, and to endeavor to make themselves known. But who would believe that a mean stork was the renowned calif Chasid? And even if it were believed, would the inhabitants of Bagdad allow themselves to be governed by a prince of so strange an appearance?

Thus they wandered many days, barely subsisting upon wild fruits, which they could scarcely swallow on account of their long beaks. As to the lizards and frogs which their new companions were so fond of, they thought them scarcely suitable for a royal diet, and moreover they feared the results of such articles of food in their stomach. The only pleasure left them in their sad situation, was the faculty of flying, which they with the rest had so dearly bought; so they often flew to the high towers of Bagdad, to see what was going on in the city.

The first time that they resorted there, the people collected in the streets, exhibited a scene of great disquietude mixed with deep grief. This rent the heart of the poor vizier. But the fourth day after

their transformation, as our two birds were just
lighting upon a tower in the calif's palace, behold !
suddenly they perceived a magnificent procession,
which marched through the streets to the joyous
flourish of trumpets and drums. Mounted upon a
horse splendidly equipped, which Chasid recognized,
under its velvet trappings, as his own favorite animal, a man clothed in a scarlet cloak, embroidered
with gold, rode triumphantly, surrounded with a
body-guard in brilliant costumes, and half of Bagdad
bowed before him, crying, " Hail, Mezia ! hail to the
king of Bagdad !"

At this moment the two storks, who were perched
upon the top of the palace, looked at each other,
and Chasid spoke :

" Do you not now understand the cause of our
transformation, grand vizier ?  This Mezia is the
son of my deadliest enemy, the powerful magician
Kaschnur, who in an evil hour swore an implacable
hatred against me.  But I have not yet lost all
hope.  Let us go to the tomb of the Prophet, and
perhaps the influence of that sacred place will be
able to break the charm."

The two storks then left the tower of the palace,
and set out for the coast of Medina.

The poor birds did their best to regulate their
flying with each other, but this was not easy, for
they had had so little practice.

" My lord," sighed the grand vizier, after a couple

of hours, " pardon me, but I can not hold myself up
any longer ; you fly too high for me.   It is already
late, and it will be prudent, I think, to seek a resting place for the night."

Chasid was a kind prince ; he heard with a com-
passionate ear the entreaty of his grand vizier, and
immediately he directed his flight to some ruins
which they had just discovered at the bottom of the
valley.

This place which our two birds sought, had for-

merly been occupied as a vast castle.   Beautiful and
lofty columns, which rose here and there in the
midst of the ruins, and many parlors still well preserved, bore witness to the former magnificence of
the place.   Chasid and his companion were wander-

ing around a labyrinth of immense corridors, seeking
some little place for a shelter, when suddenly the
stork Manzour stood still as if petrified.

"Master," whispered the vizier, in a faint voice,
"if it were not very foolish for a prime minister,
and still more for a stork to be afraid of phantoms,
I would confess that I am really frightened ; something has breathed and groaned near us."

The calif stopped to listen, and heard a light sob,
which seemed to come from a human being rather
than from an animal.   Full of anxiety, he wished to
proceed immediately to the place whence these
plaintive sounds issued, but the prudent vizier catching him by the end of his wing entreated him not to
rush into new and unknown dangers.   But in vain.
The calif, who bore a brave heart under the plumage
of a stork, tore himself from the beak of his vizier,
and, without hesitation, plunged headlong into a
dark corridor.

He was not delayed by a gate which seemed simply closed, and beyond which came to him still more
distinctly the repeated sobs and groans.   Chasid
continued resolutely to advance, but he had scarcely
entered the gate, when surprise chained him to the
threshold.

In one of the chambers in the ruin which was
lighted by a little grated window, he just perceived,
retired in the remotest corner, an enormous owl.
Large tears stood in her great yellow eyes, and sti-

fled sobs escaped from her crooked beak. But in spite of the grief which seemed to overwhelm her, she could not refrain from uttering a cry of joy at the sight of the calif and his companion who had rejoined him. She gracefully wiped away, with her spotted wings, the tears which filled her eyes, and to the great astonishment of the two adventurers, she cried out in good Arabic—

" Welcome, dear birds ; you are to me the delightful presage of my speedy deliverance, for it was once predicted that storks should bring great happiness to me."

As soon as the calif had recovered from the surprise which the sight of this strange apparition had
caused, he bowed courteously with his long beak,
and raising himself as well as he could upon his
slender legs, he replied,

" Madam owl, after what you have said, I think
I am not mistaken in seeing in you a person whose
misfortunes seem to have much resemblance to our
own. But, alas ! the hope which you cherish of obtaining your deliverance through us, seems to me in
vain ; and you may shortly know for yourself the extent of our helplessness, if you will deign to listen to
our history."

The owl having politely entreated him to relate it,
the calif, who prided himself upon his fine speaking,
commenced the relation of his misfortunes, with
which we are already acquainted.

## CHAPTER IV.

WHEN the calif had finished his story, the owl
thanked him for his kindness, and said to him,
" Hear now my history, and see if my misfortune is
not fully equal to yours. My father is one of
the most powerful kings of India, and I, his only
and too unfortunate daughter, was formerly called
the Princess Lusa. The same magician who trans-
formed you, also plunged me into my misfortune.
Relying upon the terror which his infamous science

usually inspires, he dared to come one day to my father's court, and to demand me in marriage for his son Mirza. Indignant at such audacity from a vile juggler, my father commanded the wretch to be thrown from the top of the palace. Kaschnur escaped, but he swore to be revenged.

"A little while afterward the wretch, who could change his appearance according to his wish, glided in unperceived among the persons who waited upon me, and one summer's evening, as I was walking in my garden with the intention of taking some refreshments, he, concealed under the garb of a slave presented to me some kind of beverage, I know not what, which quickly caused in me this frightful change.

"I had fainted. When I recovered consciousness, I was in this condition, and I heard the horrible voice of the magician crying in my ears :

"'You shall remain thus to the end of your life, disfigured, hideous, a terror even to animals themselves, at least until some one is found, who of his own free will, and in spite of your repelling appearance, shall consent to marry you. Thus I am revenged upon you and your haughty father.'

"Since that time many months have passed ; and the sad victim of an infamous magician, I have wandered in these solitary ruins, an object of aversion and disgust to everything that lives. Oh ! if I could but enjoy the sight of beautiful nature ! but, alas! I am blind during the day, and it is only when the silver moon sheds upon the earth her faint light that my eyes are freed from the thick vail that covers them."

The owl finished speaking, and again wiped her eyes with the end of her wings, for the relation of her misfortunes caused her tears again to flow.

While the princess was speaking, the calif had fallen into a deep reverie.

"If I am not mistaken," said he, "there is a common link between us unfortunate beings, but how shall we find the key to this enigma?"

"My lord," replied the owl, "I think the same I have already told you, that long ago, a kind of magician predicted that a stork should bring great happiness to me at some future time.   Well! I believe I have an idea which might assist us in escaping from this frightful labyrinth."

"Explain yourself," cried the calif, anxiously.

"The magician who has caused our misfortunes comes once a month to these ruins.   Not far from here is a spacious parlor, where he and his friend assemble for their nightly revels.   I have very often watched them there.   It may happen, said I to myself suddenly, that during some of these times, Kaschnur may let fall from him the word you have forgotten."

"Oh, my dear princess!" exclaimed the calif, "tell me quickly, when does he come?   Where is the parlor ?" The owl hesitated a moment, and then replied.

" Do not be angry, my lord, but before I can assist you in obtaining your deliverance, I must add a condition."

" Speak, speak quickly," cried the impatient calif ; "command me, I am all ready."

" I can, as far as I am concerned, be delivered immediately, but this can not be done," added she, modestly lowering her large yellow eyes, " unless one of you shall offer me your hand."

This proposal rather disconcerted the two storks, and the calif touching the vizier with his wing, drew him aside and spoke to him.

" Grand vizier, this is a foolish business, but I depend upon your assistance in order to get ourselves out of it."

" Indeed," replied Manzour, " my beloved wife would be vexed enough when I should return home ; and besides, I am an old man ; but you, my lord, you are young and unmarried, you are just the one for a handsome young princess."

" Ah, that's the difficulty," said the calif, leaning upon his wing. " How do you know that she is young and handsome ? We shall buy a pig in a poke, as they say."

They conversed together some time ; finally, when the calif perceived that his grand vizier would rather remain forever a stork than to marry the owl,

he resolved himself to fulfill the condition she im-
posed.

Transported with joy at this assurance, the **owl**
confessed to them that they could not have arrived at
**a more** seasonable time, for in **truth the** magician
and his friends would come that very night to their
accustomed place of meeting ; so, leaving their retreat, she guided the birds toward the spot where
their fate would be decided.

After having followed her a few moments through
a gloomy corridor, a brilliant light suddenly shone
through a broken wall.  The owl then recommended the two birds to keep a strict silence, and they all
continued carefully to advance as far as the opening
through which the light gleamed, **and which was**
large enough **to allow them to observe at a distance
all that was transpiring on** the **other side.**

**In the** center of **a** vast parlor, somewhat less
dilapidated than the rest of the castle, and which
was brilliantly illuminated, stood a large round table
loaded with meats and wines of all sorts.  Eight
men splendidly dressed, sat around this table, reclining upon rich sofas ; and the hearts of the two
storks beat loudly, when they recognized among
them the pretended merchant who had **sold them**
the magic powder.

The feast continued a long time.  The night was
almost spent, and our two unfortunate friends heard
nothing which related to them.  They began to

despair. Half of the guests were sleeping, and the other half, wearied with eating and drinking, were preparing to do the same, when the neighbor of the pretended merchant touched him on his elbow, saying,—

"Well, Kaschnur, tell us of your last exploits, what have you been doing for us?"

The latter, without more entreaties, immediately related a long list of infamous deeds, among which was the history of the calif and his vizier.

"And what was the word that you gave them?" interrupted the magician.

"A paltry Latin word," replied the latter, laughing at his own exploits; "and moreover one which is not easily remembered: MUTABOR."

## CHAPTER V.

TRANSPORTED with joy at having regained this unfortunate word, the storks hastened toward the entrance of the ruins with such rapidity, that the owl could scarcely follow them. The calif, however, turning to her as she joined them, said to her in a tender voice, "Thou who hast been indeed our deliverer, generous owl, receive my hand as a token of my lasting gratitude for the service you have done for us."

The calif and the vizier both together turned toward the east. Three times their long necks

bowed toward the sun, whose rays were just illumi-
nating the tops of the mountains. At length the
magic **word** MUTABOR burst from their beaks, and
they were changed into men !

Incapable of speaking, so great was their joy, **the
master** and his servant gazed **at each** other with
astonishment. They fell into each **other's** arms
weeping and laughing at the same **time.**

But who can describe their surprise when, looking
around, they perceived a beautiful young maiden,
richly dressed, standing by their side. She advanced,
smiling, and holding out her hand to the calif.
" You do not recognize any longer your poor owl !"
said she. She was so charming, that the calif,
struck **with her grace** and beauty, could not refrain
**from declaring, as he fell upon his knees, that he
regarded his** having **been a stork as** the greatest
happiness **of** his life, since it was owing **to** that
transformation that he had met with her.

The return of the calif to Bagdad, with his faithful Manzour, was welcomed by the people with
unanimous joy. But all the testimonies of affection which surrounded them, only increased the
hatred of Chasid and the vizier against the perfidious
Mirza. They advanced hastily to the palace, and
took the old magician **and** his son prisoners. By
the order of the calif, the old man was conducted to
the same place where he had imprisoned the owl,
and was there hung from the top of the highest

tower. As for the son, who was ignorant of all the evil deeds of his father, the calif gave him his choice to die or to take a pinch of snuff.

"Do you use it?" said the vizier to him with a most laughable air, as he presented the snuff-box to him, while on the other side a slave held a drawn sabre, ready to strike at the least signal.

Mirza hastily plunged his fingers into the magic box. A large pinch, accompanied with an emphatic MUTABOR, caused him in the twinkling of an eye to be changed into a fine, large stork, and the poor bird being shut up in a huge cage, was carried to the calif's gardens, where he served a long time for the amusement of the loungers of Bagdad.

Chasid and the princess, his wife, lived many long and happy years together; but the happiest moments of the calif were those when his grand vizier came every day to see him at noon.

Often on his arrival, he would relate their strange adventure, and when the calif was in a jovial humor, he would amuse himself by imitating the grand vizier, and mimicking his gait as a stork. With bent neck and stiff legs, he would march slowly around the room, clapping and fluttering his wings; then he would imitate the wo-begone appearance of the poor vizier, when he was vainly bowing toward the east, endeavoring to cry MU—MU—MU.

This trick was every time a new amusement for the calif's wife and children. But if Chasid clapped and fluttered **his wings and bowed** and cried MU— MU—MU— **too long a time, the** grand vizier, piqued at last at **the foolish** figure which his master presented of him, threatened to reveal to the princess, his wife, the contention which they had formerly between them who should marry the poor owl.

The calif then ceased, but could not be prevented from commencing again on the morrow in spite of the good vizier's threats, which however were never followed by any disastrous results.

## THE NEW SKATES.

THE PLEASURES OF WINTER.

"I DO hope the canal will freeze over to-night, so that I can try my new skates in the morning,' said Freddy Holland, one cold evening to his schoolmates.

"It's cold enough to freeze anything, I should think ; but have you new skates ?"

"Yes ; father bought me a beautiful pair this morning ; come home with me, and I'll show them to you."

"Agreed ! boys, let's all go home by Mr. Holland's, and see Fred's new skates !"

"Well, I will for one,"—and I for two," said another ; and so on, laughing and shouting, the troop of boys drew up in front of Mr. Holland's handsome residence.

"Now for a sight of the new skates!"

"Just let me put my books in the house, and then I'll bring them out to you," said Fred. "I know you will all say they are well worth looking at."

"Oh! but they are grand ones;" was the universal exclamation when Fred. reappeared with his skates. "Why, I never saw any like them!"

"No, they are a new kind; Mr. Smith unpacked them last night; father bought the very best pair from the lot, and he picked out the highest-priced pair, too; how glad I felt when I saw them!"

"Well, if they ain't just the nicest skates that ever were seen; they must have cost a great deal, though!"

"Father never buys a poor article; and there is not another such a pair of skates nearer than New York city," said Fred., boastingly.

"Oh, if Mr. Smith received a lot of them, I guess there are others as good as yours," said Jemmy Fritz, laughing.

"I tell you there ain't; the others are very nice, but these cost a half a dollar more than any of them."

"You always think your things a little better than other people's; how much are the others?"

"Different prices—two dollars, a dollar and a half, and some a dollar and a quarter."

"I've got a dollar and a quarter, of my own money—I mean to have a pair of them!"

"I mean to coax father to get me a pair."

"Father has promised me a new pair this winter; I hope he will get them to-night."

"I mean to have a pair before this time to-morrow."

Just then two men passed by, and one said to the other, "It is stinging cold, to-night; I think the canal will be closed before morning."

"Good news!" cried Fred., clapping his hands.

"I tell you what it is, boys, let all of us who can raise skates, meet on the ice right after breakfast, and skate till school-time."

"Well, that will be fine."

"You will come, won't you, Edwin?"

"I wish I could," replied Edwin sadly, "but I haven't any skates."

"Can't your father get you a pair?" asked one of the boys.

"He hasn't any father," said another, compassionately. "Hasn't he? I didn't know that."

All the boys felt so sorry for Edwin, that they did not care to talk about their skating any longer. They wanted to say something to comfort him, but, boy-like, they did not know how; so they separated for their different homes, each one thinking how hard it was for a little boy to have no father, to buy him skates and other nice things.

"Oh, those beautiful skates!" thought Edwin, as he walked slowly home, "I do wish I had a pair; I

wonder if mother couldn't get **them** ?"   But when
he went to the house, and saw his **mother** toiling
over her **sewing to** get them needful food, he felt
that it **would** be useless **to ask** her.   "**I** wonder if
there **is no** other way in which I **can** get them,"
thought he ; and long after he had gone **to bed that
night, he** lay tossing and wondering to himself
**whether** he could not earn the money **to** buy them.
The next morning he called at Mr. Smith's store to
look at the skates, and saw a pair for a dollar and a
half, which he thought just as good as those over
which Freddy had boasted so.   " Nice article that,"
said Mr. Smith ; " is just about the right size for you."

" Mr. Smith," Edwin began, and then he cleared
his throat two or three times before he could **get on ;**
" **Mr. Smith, is there** any way **in** which I can earn
money **enough to pay for these ?**"

" Why, **yes ; the boy that I had** here to run of
errands, and carry home parcels, is sick ; if you
choose to come and take his place, you can earn them
in a few days."

" I should like to, but mother wishes me to go to
school."

" And you wish the skates ?"

" Yes, sir."

" Well, if you will come to me a couple of hours
in the morning, and again in the evening when
school is done, you shall have the skates in two
weeks.   Do you think your mother can let you ?"

"I guess so, sir; I'll go home and ask her."

His mother readily gave her permission, when she saw how anxious her little boy was to get the skates. So Edwin began to get up very early in the morning, that he might finish all his mother wanted done by breakfast-time, **and** be ready to go and work for Mr. Smith immediately after.

A hopeful spirit makes a light foot, and Edwin was so quick in doing errands that Mr. Smith was greatly pleased with him, and in about three days said, "Edwin, to-morrow **is Saturday**; if **you** will come and help me all day, you shall have the skates to take home with you. My other boy **will** be back next week. Edwin's eyes glistened as he ran home to tell his mother the good news. He heard the shouts of the boys on the canal (for it was now a fine skating-place,) and said to himself, "To-morrow night at this time I'll be with them, and as happy as a king with my new skates, all my own earning!" He found his mother busy preparing something for his grandmother's rheumatism, and as the old lady groaned out with the pain in her shoulder, she said, "I am afraid I shall always have it, until I can **get a** warm shawl to wear in cold weather."

"Do put on your black one," said his mother.

"Oh, no, I hope to get to church again, when spring comes, and must keep that shawl decent to wear there. Besides, it is not thick enough to keep off rheumatism ; a little blanket shawl would be the thing."

"I know it, **and I must** try and **get you** one very soon."

"Hasn't grandmother any warm shawl?" asked Edwin.

"No."

"How much **would** it cost, mother?"

"About a dollar **and** a half."

"Just the price **of** my skates," thought the boy, "how nice it would be for me to give her a shawl! How I should enjoy to see her wear it, and in thinking I had helped to keep away her rheumatism! But then, **I** should have to go without the skates ; all the other boys **have** them, **and it would be so** pleasant to **go with** them **to the canal** to-morrow **night. Shall I give** up all **my pleasure** or not? I'll think **about it."** **He did** think—not only that night, but all the next day while doing errands. When he had carried home the last parcel for his employer, he went back to get his pay ; and when that gentleman laid down the skates, saying, "There they are, my boy, all your own—may you have many a merry time with them," his **heart** swelled with joy for **a** moment, to think that **he** owned the long coveted skates. But **then he re-**membered his grandmother, and though **the** tears **sprung** to his eyes, he said **in a** tolerably steady voice, "Would you as lief, sir, that I should take one of those blanket shawls instead of the skates?"

" A blanket shawl ! what in the world would you do with it ?"

" Give it to my grandmother, sir."

" What sudden change is this ? I thought you were half crazy for a pair of skates ?"

" So I was, but I heard grandmother say last night she could never get well of the rheumatism, until she had a warm shawl."

" And you are going to treat her to one, ha ?"

" I should like to."

" Very well, select the nicest shawl in the store. There, what do you think of that drab one ?"

" Just the thing for grandmother, but have I earned as much as that ?"

" Yes, and more too—a boy so thoughtful of his grandmother's comfort," he replied, as he carefully wrapped up the shawl.

" Thank you, sir," said Edwin leaving the store with the parcel in his hand. He did not dare to give another look at the skates ; for somehow they had never seemed so attractive as then. When he passed near the canal, he whistled loud, that he should not hear the shouts of the merry skaters ; but in spite of himself, his eyes filled with tears as he remembered he had no skates. But when he entered the house, and slipping up to his grandmother, spread a shawl round her shoulders, he had to laugh at her look of surprise. "Oh, what a nice, warm shawl !" she kept saying over and over again ;

"what a fine thing to keep off rheumatism! If I had such a shawl as that, I should be made up for life!"

"Be 'made up' then, grandmother," he said merrily, "the shawl is yours and nobody's else."

"Mine?" asked the old lady in amazement.

"Yes, yours; I earned it by going on errands for Mr. Smith, and I want you to wear it for my sake, grandmother."

"Dear heart, may the Lord bless you, and raise up as kind children to cherish you in your old age!" and she laid her trembling hand upon his head, while her lips moved as if in prayer for him.

Never had grandmother looked so well as on that evening, wrapped in Edwin's shawl. She seemed so comfortable and happy, that he was more than paid for his sacrifice. "And you gave up your skates, Edwin, for this!" said his mother, following him to his little bed-room. "Grandmother needed the shawl so much more, mother."

"My darling son!" was all she could say; but she resolved in heart that her child should have a pair of skates, too, if she had to sew all night to get them. She did not know that God had put it into the hearts of some other friends to give them to him, and that her extra toil would not be required.

On Sunday, Edwin felt very happy, seeing his grandmother in her warm shawl, and he thought to himself, "If I had the skates I could not enjoy

them to-day ; but grandmother can use her shawl
all the time.   I am glad I got it."

"That is a fine little lad of Widow Merrick's,"
said Mr. Smith to some gentlemen who were in his
store Saturday night ; "a manly little fellow," he
repeated, and then he told them the story of the
skates and shawl.

"The good boy ! he shall have a pair of skates,
for he deserves them if ever a lad did ;" and money
was quickly produced to pay for the very best skates
in the store.

On Monday morning, when Edwin was in the
yard sawing wood, a boy came up, and handed him
a parcel on which was written, "For Master Edwin
Merrick, from some friends who heard with pleasure
of his generous conduct to his grandmother, and who
feel that, though men, they might learn a lesson of
self-denial from a boy."

Edwin tore open the papers hastily, and shouted
for joy when he saw the skates !

## LITTLE ALICE.

### A STORY FOR CHRISTMAS.

DECEMBER.

SOME few winters ago, I was invited by a friend to be present at a party on Christmas Eve, given to a number of children in the family. Of course I

accepted, for nothing gives me more pleasure than
to see young and happy beings meet together.  The
evening was clear and cold, the ground was covered
with a crisp snow, and the heavens were studded
with bright stars.  It was a beautiful night, worthy
to herald the coming morrow.  It was on such a
night, doubtless, that the shepherds were keeping
watch over their flocks, when the angel of the Lord
appeared to them and told them "of the good
tidings of great joy which shall be to all people."

The house was brilliantly lighted, and the sound
of merry voices greeted me when I entered the room
where the children were busy at various games.

"Oh, do you know, aunt Anna," said one, "that
we are to have a Christmas tree to-night? and that
we are all going to get something from it?  Won't
it be beautiful?"

"Beautiful, indeed, I have no doubt," I replied.

At length a little bell rang, and the folding-doors
were thrown open, and there, before the wondering
eyes of the children, stood a beautiful Christmas
tree.  The apartment contained no light but that
shed by numerous colored wax tapers, which were
fastened among the branches of the evergreen tree,
that was completely loaded with all sorts of pretty
nick-nacks.  High over all, stood a figure of Santa
Claus, holding in his hand a flag, upon which appeared, in letters of gold, the inscription, "I wish
you all a merry Christmas, little children."  It is

impossible to describe the delight of all as they gazed for a moment in silent astonishment upon the beautiful sight, but soon their joy burst forth in words, and many were the exclamations and loud clapping of tiny hands that followed.

I had taken my seat somewhat behind the tree, that I might gaze upon the faces before me. One of these particularly attracted my attention. It was that of a little girl about eight years old, and I did not remember to have ever seen her before. She was dressed in deep mourning, and her light hair fell in luxuriant curls over her neck. She was very pale, and her blue eyes were raised earnestly, nay, almost sadly, towards the richly loaded Christmas tree. But soon her face brightened up, and she raised her little hands, and made a motion with them as if some pretty toy had caught her eye, and she would like to possess it.

At length the gifts were all distributed, and the children scattered here and there, were talking together, and showing what beautiful things they had received. At the other side of the room, quietly seated upon a low stool, is the little girl in black. Her presents are lying carelessly at her side, and she leans her cheek upon her hand, and gazes at the happy beings before her. I crossed the room to address her, but just then little Mary, a little girl three years old, came along, and stopped before her in child-like wonder, and said,—

"Don't you like your pretty things?"

I listened to hear what the other would reply, but she merely made a slight, quick motion with her hand, while the child gazed at her in astonishment.

"Well," continued Mary, quite reprovingly, "why don't you speak? You are very naughty if you don't like them," and the little one was turning hastily away, when a tear fell upon her fat hand, that had rested upon the **arm of the** other, and immediately **her** tender **feelings were** moved, and she added, as she kissed the weeping child,—

"Well, don't cry; please **don't cry.**" Turning to me, she said,—

"**Please try and make the little** girl speak."

I asked this **young** stranger a number of **questions,** to none of which, however, she made any reply. My suspicions were now aroused, and I thought, can it be that those pale lips *cannot* frame a sound? While I sat by her side, her hand clasped in mine, and her face hidden **in my** lap, a lady came smiling **towards** me, and **laying her** hand **upon** the child's head, said,—

"So you have taken my little **girl under your** charge?"

The child started, glanced hastily up, and again those delicate fingers moved quickly in the air. The lady who had addressed me, I knew to be the matron **of the** neighboring deaf **and** dumb asylum. My **suspicions** were correct. It was not that this little one *would not* but that she *could not speak.*

Some years have passed, and I often visit the asylum where Alice Manning is being educated. By practice, I have, myself, become quite well acquainted with the language of signs, and it is one of my greatest pleasures to sit by the side of that sweet and affectionate mute, and converse with her, through the medium of our fingers.   By education, her whole character is rapidly improving.   She is becoming more and more interesting, and is none the less so because she cannot speak, for her soul finds eloquent utterance in the eye and in the impressive language of signs.

## A VISIT FROM ST. NICHOLAS.

'Twas the night before Christmas, when, all through the house,
Not a creature was stirring, not even a mouse;
The stockings were hung by the chimney with care,
In hopes that St. Nicholas soon would be there;
The children were nestled all snug in their beds,
While visions of sugar-plums danced through their heads;
And mamma in her 'kerchief, and I in my cap,
Had just settled our brains for a long winter's nap—
When out on the lawn there arose such a clatter,
I sprang from the bed to see what was the matter.
Away to the window I flew like a flash,
Tore open the shutters and threw up the sash.
The moon, on the breast of the new fallen snow,
Gave the lustre of mid-day to objects below,
When, what to my wondering eyes should appear,
But a miniature sleigh and eight tiny reindeer,
With a little old driver, so lively and quick,
I knew in a moment it must be St. Nick.
More rapid than eagles his coursers they came,
And he whistled, and shouted, and called them by name:
" Now, Dasher! now, Dancer! now, Prancer! now, Vixen!
On, Comet! on, Cupid! on, Donder and Blixen!
To the top of the porch! to the top of the wall!
Now, dash away, dash away, dash away all!"
As leaves that before the wild hurricane fly,
When they meet with an obstacle, mount to the sky,
So, up to the house-top the coursers they flew,
With the sleigh full of toys—and St. Nicholas too.
And then in a twinkling, I heard on the roof
The prancing and pawing of each little hoof.
As I drew in my head, and was turning around,
Down the chimney St. Nicholas came with a bound.
He was dressed all in fur, from his head to his foot,

And his clothes were all tarnish'd with ashes and soot;
A bundle of toys he had flung on his back,
And he looked like a peddlar just opening his pack;
His eyes—how they twinkled! his dimples how merry!
His cheeks were like roses, his nose like a cherry;
His droll little mouth was drawn up like a bow,
And the beard on his chin was white as the snow.
The stump of a pipe he held tight in his teeth,
And the smoke it encircled his head like a wreath.
He had a broad face, and a little round belly,
That shook, when he laugh'd, like a bowl full of jelly
He was chubby and plump; a right jolly old elf;
And I laughed when I saw him in spite of myself.
A wink of his eye, and a twist of his head,
Soon gave me to know I had nothing to dread.
He spoke not a word, but went straight to his work,
And filled all the stockings; *then turned with a jerk*,
*And laying his finger aside of his nose,*
*And giving a nod, up the chimney he rose.*
He sprang to his sleigh, to his team gave a whistle,
And away they all flew like the down of a thistle;
But I heard him exclaim, ere he drove out of sight,
" Happy Christmas to all, and to all a Good Night."

# THE LEGEND OF KING ROBERT OF SICILY.

RITERS inform us, that King Robert of Sicily, brother of Pope Urban and of the Emperor Valemond, was a prince of great valor and renown, but of a temper so proud and impatient, that he did not like to bend his knee to Heaven itself, but would sit twirling his beard, and looking with something worse than indifference round about him, during the services of the church.

Well, one day, while he was present at vespers on the eve of St. John, his attention was excited to some words in the Magnificat, in consequence of a sudden dropping of the choristers' voices. The words were these : " *Deposuit potentes de sede, et exaultavit humiles.*" (He hath put down the mighty from their seat, and hath exalted the humble.) Being far too great and warlike a prince to know anything of Latin, he asked a chaplain near

him the **meaning of these** words ; **and** being told
what it was, observed that such expressions were no
better than an old song, since men like himself were
not so **easily** pulled down, much **less supplanted** by
poor creatures whom people called "**humble.**"

The chaplain, doubtless out of pure astonishment
**and** horror, made no reply ; and his majesty, partly
**from** the heat of the weather, and partly to relieve
himself from the rest of the service, fell asleep.

After some lapse of time, the royal "sitter in the
seat of the scornful," owing, as he thought, to the
sound of the organ, but in reality to a great droning
fly in his ear, woke up in more than his usual state
of impatience ; and **he was** preparing **to** vent it,
when, to his astonishment, **he perceived the church
empty. Every soul was gone, excepting a deaf** old
woman **who was turning up the cushions. He** addressed her to no purpose : **he** spoke louder and
louder, and was proceeding, as well as rage and
amaze would let him, to try if he could walk out of
the church without a dozen lords before him, when
suddenly catching a sight of his face, the old woman
uttered a cry of "Thieves!" and shuffled away, first
closing the door behind her.

King Robert looked at the door in **silence, then**
round about him **at the** empty church, then **at him-**
self. His cloak of ermine **was** gone. The coronet
was taken from his cap. The very jewels from his
fingers. "Thieves verily!" thought the king, turn-

ing white, for shame and rage. "Here is conspiracy
—rebellion! This is that sanctified traitor, the
Duke. Horses shall tear them all to pieces. What
ho, there! Open the door for the king!"

"For the constable, you mean!" said a voice
through the keyhole. "You're a pretty fellow!"

The king said nothing.

"Thinking to escape, in the king's name," said
the voice, "after hiding to plunder his closet.
We've got you."

Still the king said nothing.

The sexton could not refrain from another jibe at
his prisoner:

"*I* see you, there," said he—"by the big lamp,
grinning like a rat in a trap. How do you like your
bacon?"

Now, whether King Robert was of the blood of
that Norman chief who felled his enemy's horse with
a blow of his fist, we know not; but certain it is,
that the only answer he made the sexton was by
dashing his enormous foot against the door, and
bursting it open in his teeth. The sexton, who felt
as if a giant had given him a blow in the face, fainted away; and the king, as far as a sense of dignity allowed him, hurried to his palace, which was
close by.

"Well," said the porter, "what do *you* want?"

"Stand aside, fellow!" roared the king, pushing
back the door, with the same gigantic foot.

" Be gone with you ;" said the porter, who was a
stout fellow too, and pushed the king back before he
expected resistance. The king, however, was too
much for him. He felled him to the ground ; and
half strode, half rushed into the palace, followed by
the exasperated janitor.

" Seize him," cried the porter.

" On your lives," cried the king. " Look at me,
fellow :—who am I ?"

" A mad beast and fool ; that's what you are,'
cried the porter ; " and you're a dead man, for coming drunk into the palace, and hitting the king's
servants. Hold him fast."

In came the guards, with an officer at their head,
who was going to visit his mistress, and had been
dressing his curls at a looking-glass. He had the
looking-glass in his hand.

" Captain Francavilla," said the king, " is the
world run mad ? or what is it ? Do your rebels
pretend not even to know me ? Go before me, sir,
to my rooms." And as he spoke, the king shook
off his assailants, as a lion does curs, and moved on-
wards.

Captain Francavilla put his finger gently before
the king to stop him ; and then looking with a sort
of staring indifference in his face, said, in a very
mild tone, " Some madman."

King Robert tore the looking-glass from the captain's hand, and looked himself in the face. *It was*

*not his own face.* It was another man's face, very hot and vulgar; and had something in it at once melancholy and ridiculous.

"By the living!" exclaimed Robert, "here is witchcraft! I am changed." And, for the first time in his life, a sensation of fear came upon him, but nothing so great as the rage and fury that remained. All the world believed in witchcraft, as well as King Robert; but they had still more certain proofs of the existence of drunkenness and madness; and the king's household had seen the king come forth from church as usual, and were ready to split their sides for laughter at the figure of this raving impostor, pretending to be King Robert *changed!*

"Bring him in—bring him in," now exclaimed other voices, the news having got to the royal apartments; "the king wants to see him."

King Robert was brought in; and there, amidst roars of laughter, (for courts were not quite such well-bred places then as they are now,) he found himself face to face with *another King Robert*, seated on his throne, and as like his former self as he himself unlike, but with more dignity.

"Hideous impostor!" exclaimed Robert, rushing forward to tear him down.

The court, at the word "hideous," roared with greater laughter than before; for the king, in spite of his pride, was at all times a handsome man; and there was a strong feeling at present that he had never in his life looked so well.

Robert, when half way to the throne, felt as if a palsy had struck him. He stopped, and essayed to vent his rage, but could not speak.

The figure on the throne looked him steadily in the face. Robert thought it was a wizard, but hated far more than he feared him, for he was of great courage.

It was an angel.

But the angel was not going to disclose himself yet, nor for a long time. Meanwhile, he behaved, on the occasion, very much like a man ; we mean, like a man of ordinary feelings and resentments, though still mixed with a dignity beyond what had been before observed in the Sicilian monarch. Some of the courtiers attributed it to a sort of royal instinct of contrast, excited by the claims of the impostor ; but others (by the angel's contrivance) had seen him, as he came out of the church, halt suddenly, with an abashed and altered visage, before the shrine of St. Thomas, as if supernaturally struck with some visitation from Heaven for his pride and unbelief. The rumor flew about on the instant, and was confirmed, by an order given from the throne, the moment the angel seated himself upon it, for a gift of a hitherto unheard-of amount to the shrine itself.

" Since thou art royal mad," said the new sovereign, "and in truth the very king of idiots, thou shalt be crowned and sceptred with a cap and bauble, and be my fool."

Robert was still tongue-tied. He tried in vain to speak—to roar out his disgust and defiance; and half mad indeed, with the inability, pointed with his quivering finger, to the inside of his mouth, as if in apology to the beholders for not doing it. Fresh shouts of laughter made his brain seem to reel within him.

"Fetch the cap and bauble," said the sovereign, "and let the king of fools have his coronation."

Robert felt that he must submit to what he thought the power of the evil one; and began to have glimpses of a real though hesitating sense of the advantage of securing friendship on the side of Heaven. But rage and indignation were uppermost; and while the attendants were shaving his head, fixing the cap, and jeeringly dignifying him with the bauble-sceptre, he was racking his brains for schemes of vengeance. What exasperated him most of all, next to the shaving, was to observe, that those who had flattered him most when a king, were the loudest in their contempt, now, that he was the court-zany. One pompous lord in particular, with a high and ridiculous voice, which continued to laugh when all the rest had done, and produced fresh peals by the continuance, was so excessively provoking, that Robert, who felt his vocal and muscular powers restored to him as if for the occasion, could not help shaking his fist at the grinning slave, and crying **out,** " Thou beast, Terranova ; " which, in **all** but the person so addressed, only produced additional merriment.   At length the king ordered the fool to be taken away, to sup with the dogs. Robert was stupefied ; but he found himself hungry against his will, and gnawed the bones which had been chucked away by his nobles.

The proud King **Robert** of Sicily lived in this way for two years, always raging in his mind, always sullen in his manners, and subjected to every indignity that his quondam favorites could heap on him, without the power to resent it, for the new monarch seemed unjust to him only.   He had all the humiliations, without **any of** the privileges, of **the cap** and bells, and was the dullest **fool ever** heard **of.**   All the notice the king took of him, consisted in asking now and then, in full court, when everything was silent, " Well, fool, art thou still a king ?"   Robert for some weeks, loudly answered that he was ; but, finding that the answer was but a signal for a roar of laughter, converted his speech into the silent dignity of a haughty and royal attitude ; till, **observ**ing the laughter to be greater at this dumb **show,** he ingeniously adopted a manner which expressed neither defiance nor acquiescence, and the angel for some time let him alone.

Meantime, everybody, but the unhappy Robert,

blessed the new, or, as they supposed him, the altered king : for everything in the mode of government was changed. Taxes were light ; the poor had
plenty ; work was reasonable ; the nobles themselves
were expected to work after their fashion—to study,
to watch zealously over the interests of their tenants,
to travel, and bring home new books and innocent
luxuries. Half the day throughout Sicily was given
to industry, and half to healthy intellectual enjoyment ; and the inhabitants became at once the man-
liest and tenderest, the gayest and most studious
people in the world. Wherever the king went, he
was loaded with benedictions ; and the fool heard
them, and began to wonder what evil spirit had con-
jured up appearances so extraordinary. And thus,
during the space of time we have mentioned, he
lived wondering, and sullen, and hating, and hated.

At the expiration of these two years, or nearly
so, the king announced his intention of paying a
visit to his brother the pope, and his brother the emperor, the latter agreeing to come to Rome for the
purpose. He went accordingly with a great train
clad in the most magnificent garments, all but the
fool, who was arrayed in fox-tails, and put side by
side with an ape, dressed like himself. The people
poured out of their houses, and fields, and vine-
yards, all struggling to get a sight of the king's
face, and to bless it, the ladies strewing flowers, and
the peasants' wives holding up their rosy children,

which last sight seemed particularly to delight the
sovereign. The fool, bewildered, came after the
court-pages, by the side of his ape, exciting shouts
of laughter, and, in some bosoms, not a little astonishment, to think how a monarch so kind and
considerate to all the rest of the world, should be
so hard upon a sorry fool.  But it was told them,
that this fool was the most perverse and insolent of
men towards the prince himself ; and then, although
their wonder hardly ceased, it was full of indignation against the unhappy wretch, and he was loaded
with every kind of scorn and abuse.  The proud
King Robert seemed the only blot and disgrace upon
the island.

The fool had still a hope, that when his holiness
the pope saw him, the magician's arts would be at
an end ; for though he had had no religion at all,
properly speaking, he had retained something even
of a superstitious faith in the worldly forms of it.
The pope, however, beheld him without the least
recognition ; so did the emperor ; and when he beheld them both gazing with unfeigned admiration at
the exalted beauty of his former altered self, and
not with the old faces of pretended good-will and secret dislike, a sense of awe and humility, for the first
time, fell gently upon him.  Instead of getting as
far as possible from his companion the ape, he approached him closer and closer, partly that he might
shroud himself under the very shadow of his insig-

nificance, partly from a feeling of absolute sympathy and a desire to possess, if not one friend in the world, at least one associate who was not an enemy.

It happened that day that it was the eve of St. John, the same on which, two years ago, Robert had heard and scorned the words in the Magnificat. Vespers were performed before the pope, and the two sovereigns : the music and the soft voices fell softer as they came to the words, and Robert again heard but with far different feelings, *Deposuit potentes de sede, et exaltavit humiles :* " He hath put down the mighty from their seat, and exalted the humble." Tears gushed into his eyes, and, to the astonishment of the court, the late sullen and brutal fool was seen with his hands reverently clasped upon his bosom in prayer, and the tears pouring down his face in floods of penitence. Something of holier feeling than usual had turned all hearts that day. The king's own favorite chaplain had preached from the text which declares charity to be greater than faith or hope. The emperor began to think that mankind were really his brethren. The pope wished that some new council of the church would authorize him to set up over the Ten Commandments, and, in more glorious letters, the new, *eleventh*, or great Christian commandment—" Behold, I give unto you a *new* commandment : LOVE ONE ANOTHER." In short, Rome felt that day like angel-governed Sicily.

When the service was over, and the sovereigns

had gone to their apartments, King Robert's behavior was reported to the unsuspected King-Angel,
who had seen it, but said nothing. The sacred in-
terloper announced his intention of giving the fool a
trial in some better office, and he sent for him accordingly, having first dismissed every other person.
King Robert came, in his fool's-cap and bells, and
stood humbly at a distance before the great unknown
looking on the floor and blushing. He had the ape
by the hand, who had long courted his good-will,
and who, having now obtained it, clung to his human
friend in a way that, to a Roman, might have seemed ridiculous, but to the angel was affecting.

" Art thou still a king ?" said the King-Angel,
putting the old question, but without the word "fool."

" I am a fool," said King Robert, " and no king."

" What wouldst thou, Robert ?" returned the angel, in a mild voice.

King Robert trembled from head to foot, and said,
" Even what thou wouldst, O mighty and good
stranger, whom I know not how to name—hardly to
look upon !"

The stranger laid his hand on the shoulder of
King Robert, who felt an inexpressible calm suddenly diffuse itself over his whole being. He knelt
down and clasped his hands to thank him.

" Not to me," interrupted the angel, in a grave
but sweet voice ; and kneeling down by the side of
Robert, he said, as if in church, " Let us pray."

King Robert prayed, and the angel prayed, and after a few moments, the king looked up, and the angel was gone ; and then the king knew that it was an angel indeed.

And his own likeness returned to King Robert, but never an atom of his pride ; and after a blessed reign, he died, disclosing this history to his weeping nobles, and requesting that it might be recorded in the Sicilian Annals.

## THE SAILOR YOUTH.

### CHAPTER I.—SORROW.

IT is a beautiful morning in the month of November. The eastern sky is filled with light, rosy clouds, and the glorious sun, bursting forth, heralds the approach of a bright, clear day. The little village of S——, where the scene of our story is laid, is situated on the extreme eastern coast of Massachusetts. The inhabitants of the place, a thriving, indus-

trious set of people, have been stirring for more than
three hours, attending to their various household duties. The place is very prettily laid out, in straight,
regular streets, bordered on each side with fine forest
trees, thus forming in the summer season delightful
shady walks. At the far end of the village, on a
slight eminence, stands the church, embedded in a
perfect grove of foliage, which has now assumed its
bright autumnal tints.

Adjoining is a cottage, occupied by the pastor and
his family. In one of the lower rooms of this dwelling a young girl of about nineteen years of age is
busily occupied arranging the breakfast-table. Her
form is slender, but well-proportioned, and her fair
skin is delicately tinged with the rosy hue of health ;
her eyes are of a dark blue, and her hair, which is
laid smoothly over her brow, is of a rich brown
color ; yet her chief charm is not in her looks, but
in her manner. Although she had been petted and
admired by many, still she is not spoiled ; no vain
or selfish feelings find harborage in her gentle heart.
*She* is, indeed, first with all ; but with her, *all* are
before herself. Such is Mary Eldridge, the pastor's
only daughter.

"There, mother," she exclaimed, as a lady o.
about forty years of age entered the apartment,
"everything is prepared for breakfast." Then she
added, as she turned toward the door of her father's
study, "Is papa ready for prayers, do you think ?"

"He has not returned home yet, my dear," replied her mother.

"Returned home! where has he gone?" she inquired in astonishment.

"Why, did not Margaret tell you?" said Mrs. Eldridge, "that they sent for him very early this morning from Mrs. Martin's, with word that her little girl was dying?"

"What, dear little Agnes!" exclaimed Mary, her eyes filling with tears. "When was she taken sick? I have heard nothing about it. It was only yesterday morning," she continued, "that I passed their house, and there, in the garden, was the little one, with her blind brother. It was a beautiful sight," she added, "to see that sweet child, only five years old, leading by the hand her brother, two years older than herself, she his guide and support."

"She will, indeed, be a great loss to him," replied the pastor's wife ; "but we should remember, Mary, that what is Willie's *loss* will be Agnes' *gain*. But there is your father," she continued, "coming along the road. Run, my child, and open the gate for him."

In an instant Mary was at the front door, and in a few moments her loved father's arm was around her, while, with his usual "God bless you!" he pressed an affectionate morning greeting upon her lips. Then her head sank upon his shoulder, and she burst into a flood of tears.

"Mary, my child, you must not weep so," he said, as he led her sobbing into the house. "It is true little Agnes has gone, and we will all miss her; but she was too pure for this earth, she was but lent to us for a short season, and now the Lord has taken her again to himself."

"What physician did they employ, Edward?" inquired his wife.

"The child was taken suddenly ill last evening," replied Mr. Eldridge, "and Mr. Martin sent off immediately for Dr. Howard," he added, turning toward his daughter, the color of whose cheeks assumed a deeper hue. "I found the Doctor there when I arrived; he had remained by the bedside of the sick child the whole night, watching every symptom, and using every means in his power to preserve life, but in vain. When I entered the apartment in which they were assembled, there, on the bed, lay the dying child, the poor mother clasping her little one's hand between her own, while, kneeling at Mrs. Martin's feet, his face buried in her lap, and sobbing as if his heart would break, was poor blind Willie. The father stood silently at the foot of the bed, by the side of the physician. When the Doctor was preparing to depart, Mrs. Martin rose, and, taking both his hands, said: 'We can not express to you how deeply thankful we feel for your kind attention to'—here her voice trembled, and she glanced toward the bed. 'You have done all that you could do,

and much more than we had a right to expect.'
The tears shone in Dr. Howard's eyes ; he could
scarcely utter a word, but after warmly pressing the
hands of both parents, and whispering a few words
of comfort to blind Willie, he turned for an instant
toward the dying one.  As he leaned over her, she
opened her eyes slightly, and murmured ' *kiss.*'  He
bent silently down, and when he raised his head a
tear-drop glistened on little Agnes' pale forehead."

As Mr. Eldridge in a low tone related the foregoing sad scene, the tears streamed from the eyes of
his wife and child, while he himself, with much
difficulty, could scarcely suppress his feelings.  After a moment's silence, he added : "it is very late,
we must have prayers now.  But where is your
brother, Mary ?  The lazy boy, has he not come
down yet ?"

"Why !" exclaimed Mrs. Eldridge, " I never
thought of Henry.  Run up stairs, my child, and
see what keeps him ; perhaps he may not be well."

As Mary turned to obey her mother, a loud
scratching was heard at the front door.  " Oh, there
is Ocean," she said.  " I will just let him in first,
for I expect the poor fellow thinks it very strange
that he has not had his breakfast yet."

She was indeed right ; for, when she opened the
door, there stood a large Newfoundland dog, who,
without stopping to receive his accustomed caress,
pushed roughly past her, and, springing into the

sitting-room, uttered a low, mournful howl, as he laid a handkerchief at his master's feet. Mr. Eldridge raised it, while his wife exclaimed immediately, " It is our son's !"

They now perceived that the dog was dripping wet. Their fears were at once roused ; perhaps in bathing, near the shore, their son had been carried out by a strong wave, and the dog had endeavored to save him, but, failing therein, had brought home his handkerchief as a token of his fate. Just as they had silently arrived at this terrible conclusion, Mary rushed into the apartment with an open letter in her hand, which she handed to her father, and, throwing herself on her knees at his side, she exclaimed, sobbing violently, " Oh ! Henry has gone ! he has gone to sea."

As her daughter uttered these words, Mrs. Eldridge sank back into her chair, while her husband hastily glanced at the contents of the letter. At last he read in a trembling voice the following lines :

MY DEAR PARENTS—I leave you thus suddenly, because I fear that mother would so oppose my going to sea, that I fear I should be obliged to give up the idea, and it has, you know, been always my most anxious desire to be a sailor. Please, dear mother, forgive your son this want of dutiful obedience toward your wishes, and believe that it is not without feelings of sorrow that I leave my home and all who are dear to me. Tell sister Mary not to forget me, and that in a few **years I** will return, and have much to tell her about the world and its wonders. I have taken the Bible that you **gave** me, mother, **when I** was but ten years old, **just** eight years ago. I will read **it, night** and morning, for your sake, and I hope it may do **me some** good. You will find, also, that **I have taken** my **small** trunk, filled with my clothes ; **it is all I** shall want. I go with one **who has the name of** being a very kind captain, but I will write and let you know all, the first port we make. Give my good-bye to all friends, but particularly to Walter Howard ; and Mary can tell him, if she chooses, that I hope to find **him** nearer than a *friend* when I return home. Now, dear father and mother, farewell, and **to be remembered night and morning in your prayers is the last wish of your ever-loving son.** H ENRY E LDRIDGE.

When Mr. Eldridge had finished **the** letter, he turned and said : " We can but trust that we will meet again." Then quietly rising from his chair, he took his **wife** and daughter by the hand, and led them into 'his study, and there the three kneeled down, while he offered up **a** prayer, in which the present and the absent, those in grief and those in joy, were all remembered by their affectionate **pastor.**

CHAPTER II.—THE VISIT.

New Year's day has arrived, and many are the preparations for feasting that are taking place in the little village of S——. Neither has their pastor been forgotten, for, on his return from church, he found his table filled to overflowing with kind gifts from his flock. But an air of sadness reigned throughout the dwelling; the inmates feel that the day is not such a one as they had expected it would be. Poor Mary! she had been making great calculations for this day. She had expected to have had her dear brother with her, and he had intended to invite to dinner his friend Walter Howard. But now all was changed, for that brother was gone, and they knew not whither.

"Mother," said Mary, after they had finished their silent meal, "I believe I will go this afternoon and see Mrs. Martin; she may think it strange that I have not called before."

"She will be very glad to see you, my dear, I do not doubt," replied her mother, "but she thinks nothing of it; for I told her this morning at church that you had been sick for the last few weeks, and she said something about coming to see you herself."

"Dear, good woman!" exclaimed Mary. "And I will carry some fresh eggs," she added, "to blind Willie, he loves them so much. Sweet boy, he can not say now, as he used to do, whenever I gave him anything, "Agnes shall have some too."

Immediately rising she filled a basket with some nice new-laid eggs, and, putting on her simple straw hat, and throwing a shawl over her shoulders, after kissing both her parents affectionately, she left the house and turned her steps toward Mrs. Martin's dwelling. This was some distance from Mr. Eldridge's, and part of the way lay through quite a wood, where, in summer, it was Mary's great delight to roam, gathering wild flowers, with which to adorn her father's study. As she drew near the cottage, she perceived, seated in his accustomed seat on the front steps, the little blind boy. When she opened the gate he started, listened to the sound, and the instant her foot touched the gravel walk he recognized her step, and murmuring, "Miss Mary," burst into a flood of tears.

"Dear Willie," she exclaimed, as she stooped down and kissed his pale cheek, "you must not cry so."

"Why do *you* cry ?" said the child as he raised his sightless eyes, and pointed toward his hand on which she had let fall more than one tear. He *felt*, though could not *see*.

"I cry to see you so unhappy," she answered. Then placing herself by his side, and taking one of his hands in hers, she continued in a soothing tone, "Listen to me, Willie. You had a dear little sister, but the good God, who gave her to you, saw fit to take her away, and you should not grieve so, since it was his will."

"But she will never lead me about again," he exclaimed, still weeping bitterly.

" Not till God calls you, also, to himself, dear ; then you will meet your lost sister, and there, in a more beautiful and brighter world than this, she will lead you to Jesus' feet."

" And shall I *see* all that beautiful world ? and shall I *see* Agnes then, Miss Mary ?" inquired the blind boy, earnestly.

" Yes, Willie," she replied, " you will *see* them."

" Oh ! I should be so happy to die now !" answered the child ; " why don't God call me ?   But he never has yet, has he ?   I would have heard him, wouldn't I ?" he added anxiously, " though I did not hear him when he called sister Agnes."

" No, Willie, you did not hear him, but Agnes did.   But you must not wish to die till you are called for—that is not right.   Come, let us go into the house now," she continued, " and see your mamma ; and here are some fresh eggs ; carry them to Ellen and ask her to take them out."

The child took the basket, but his heart was too full to utter his thanks for the nice present ; his thoughts were with that loved sister, with whom he had always shared all such gifts.   The meeting between the bereaved mother and our young friend was solemn and affecting.   After sitting an hour or two with Mrs. Martin, Mary rose to leave, saying, as they stood together upon the steps, " See, the sun has set ! it is quite late, and it will be dark before I get home."

"But you have nothing to be afraid of in our quiet village," replied Mrs. Martin, "only the walk will be lonesome for you. I wish my husband were here, and then he could accompany you."

'Oh, that would not be worth while," replied Mary, adding, as she kissed her for good-bye, "perhaps I may overtake some of the neighbors on the road."

Then, with her empty basket hanging on her arm, she took her way toward home. When she reached the woods, the road through which was not quite dark, she suddenly heard a quick step behind her, and a voice exclaimed, "Good-evening, Miss Mary!" She turned, for she had immediately recognized the tones, and in an instant Doctor Howard was standing at her side. Arm-in-arm the two now walked quietly toward Mr. Eldridge's cottage, and as they parted at the gate, the Doctor pressed a kiss upon her rosy lips, and she did not attempt to resent this liberty, but quietly submitted. They seemed to understand one another very well.

### CHAPTER III.—THE SHIPWRECK.

Six years have passed away. It is New Year's eve. The clouds are dark and heavy, and the rising wind betokens that there will be a severe storm during the night.

The old familiar sitting-room in Mr. Eldridge's cottage is brightly lighted up, a cheerful fire burns in the grate, and happy is the party there assembled, for the old man's family has quite increased since we last saw him. There he sits at one side of the table reading, and looking as hale as ever, while opposite to him is his wife, occupied with her knitting. Near her mother stands our friend Mary, holding a sleeping infant in her arms, while a little boy of about four years of age is lying on the floor, engaged in tormenting, in various childlike ways, a large Newfoundland dog, who is stretched lazily out by his side. In one corner of the room there is seated, on a low stool, a lad of about twelve years of age, busily employed in weaving a basket. It is blind Willie. He is now an orphan, and since the death of his parents he has found a kind home at the parsonage.

"Come, my child," said Mary, addressing the little urchin at her feet; "it is time for you to go to bed. Agnes is sound asleep," she added, glancing at the babe.

"Oh, please let me stay up, mamma, till papa comes home," he replied, as he pulled the dog's long, black ears.

"No, my dear; you must come now, for your papa may not be home till very late; and I expect Ocean will be glad to get rid of you, for you have not given him a moment's peace for the last hour."

The child laughed, patted the animal lovingly on the head, saying, "Good-night, Ocean!" Then, after receiving an affectionate embrace from his grandfather and grandmother, and kissing Willie, he followed his mother, though somewhat unwillingly, from the room. When her children were safe in bed, Mary returned to the sitting-room, and quietly seated herself at her work. She had not been there many minutes, before the door of the apartment was thrown open, and Doctor Howard entered.

" Why, what has made you so late, Walter ?" she exclaimed, rising, and attempting to take off his overcoat, which was dripping wet, for the rain by this time was pouring down in torrents.

" I could not help it, Mary," he replied, kissing her cheek ; " I have had so much to attend to, and now I must go out again immediately."

" You are not going out during this terrible storm ?" inquired his wife, as she glanced anxiously from the window into the dark street, which was, at short intervals, made light as day by the vivid streaks of lightning that flashed over the whole heavens, followed by the most fearful peals of thunder.

" Yes," replied her husband ; " it is necessary, for I have just met one of our neighbors, and he tells me that there is a ship off the coast in distress, and that the people are assembling to try and assist her, so I merely stopped to tell you all not to be uneasy about me. I will return as soon as I possibly can. Come, Ocean !" he added, whistling to the dog ;

"you may be of some use." At this call the animal
rose, shook his long, shaggy hair, and as Willie
patted him on the back, saying, "See now, old
fellow, if you can't save some poor sailor's life," he
trotted quickly after his master.

A ship in distress! What mingled emotions
stirred the hearts of this little family! They
thought of that son who so many years before had
left them so unexpectedly, and whom they had never
heard from since. Perhaps in some far distant port,
the vessel in which he sailed was also in distress,
and there were none near to offer assistance; or
perhaps he had already found a grave in that watery
deep where many others might be resting with him
before to-morrow's sun arose.

We will now follow Doctor Howard and his canine
companion. When they reached the shore, the
former instantly perceived by the flashes of lightning that, at a short distance from the coast, was a
large vessel laboring through the water, and in imminent danger of being dashed to pieces against the
rocks which were hidden beneath the white waves.
The bank was crowded with people, some proposing
one thing, and some another; but as soon as Walter
Howard appeared, they all turned toward him, and
inquired what means he would advise as the best to
be used toward saving these poor, helpless beings.
He immediately ordered a long rope to be secured at
one end to the stern of a boat which was lying up on

the sand ; the other end of it he placed in the hands of one of the men, and then pushing the skiff into the water and stepping into it, he turned toward a tall, sturdy fisherman **who** was standing near, and hastily inquired, " Will you accompany **me**, George ?"

The man **made no reply,** except by springing quickly in after him.    Then he seemed **to** hesitate, and Walter Howard thought for an instant that he was unwilling perhaps to run so great a risk ; but he merely turned toward the shore, and addressing the assembled people, who had stood silently watching their movements, in a loud voice said, " Is there none here who have courage to accompany me, **and** let the Doctor remain on land ?    He has a family, **and there are many of you who, like myself, are alone in the** world."    Hardly had he uttered these words, than they crowded toward the boat, all willing to risk their lives in the place of one who was so universally beloved.    But their generous and ready offers were not to be accepted, for Walter Howard with one of the oars hastily pushed the boat out into the rough waters, exclaiming, " No, no, I will go myself, though I thank you all.    I trust all will go well.    Attend to the rope, hold it securely, and if we call to you to draw in, do so," he added, as they pushed farther out into the deep.

Thrice did that little boat, by the efforts of these noble men, journey from the land to the sinking vessel, each time returning laden with a heavy load of thankful beings. When they reached the shore for the third time, the fisherman sprang upon the beach, then touching Walter Howard respectfully upon the arm, he exclaimed, as he pointed out toward the dark waters, " We must not return again."

" Oh, George !" replied the other, " there are but a few more men on board. I do not believe the vessel will sink before we can get them off. Come, go with me once more !"

" Doctor Howard," replied the man, " we might possibly, although I doubt it, have time to reach the ship again, but we would never," he added, earnestly, " when *there, return.*"

His fears were but too true ; for hardly had these words passed his lips, when the lightning flashed brightly over the wreck. It was heaving its last throes ; screams of agony reached the ears of the anxious spectators ; then a heavy, sudden splash sounded in the deep waters, and all was silent as death, both on land and sea ; even the tempest seemed for an instant to hush its fury.

The Doctor now placed himself upon a rock overhanging the shore, and by his side stood the faithful Ocean. The former is anxiously watching for the appearance of any bodies that may be thrown toward the land. Suddenly the animal at his feet stretches his black head out in the direction of the water ; then, giving a low, long whine, springs into

the waves beneath, and strikes boldly out toward a
dark object, which is dashed helplessly about by the
raging storm.  The dog has reached it, and grasp-
ing it securely between his teeth, he turns, and in a
few moments drags upon the sand the body of a
sailor.  Now the animal moans sadly, gazes as if
he would almost speak into the many faces that
crowd around ; then he stoops over the body and
licks the pale, wet face.

"How strange the dog acts !" exclaims the fisherman whom we have called George.  "Can it be
any one he knows ?  Doctor," he added, as he held
a lantern toward the ground, "see if you can recognize him."

Walter Howard bent forward, and as the light
flickered over the features of the unconscious man,
he started back, uttering the words : "Good heavens !  It is Henry Eldridge !"

Great indeed was the anxiety and excitement,
when the crowd learned that it was the son of their
respected pastor ; and not many minutes had elapsed
before he was carried in their arms into a neighboring cottage, where his brother-in-law used every
means in his power to revive him.  His efforts were
not fruitless, for before half an hour had passed, the
young man showed evident signs of recovery.  Old
Ocean had stood quietly during all this time at the
foot of the bed ; but when he saw his master Henry
open his eyes, the dog snatched something from off
a chair, and started unobserved out of the room.

circumstances to let him go to the one in the neighboring town.

Attached to her little cottage was about an acre of ground. This Joe used to cultivate, raising potatoes, cabbages, tomatoes, and various other vegetables, for which he found a ready sale, besides having enough left for their own use during the winter.

It grieved Joe very much to think he was debarred the high privilege of getting an education. He was very ambitious to be great and rich. Of a visionary turn of mind, all his leisure moments, during the long days of summer, were spent building castles in the air, each to crumble to decay among the ruins of the past.

He was passionately fond of the water, and had a great desire to become a sailor, and travel over the boundless ocean ; and, if he had had no one but himself to consult, he would have, ere this, found the ship-board, and sailed before the mast.

But the dearest of all earthly ties held him back. That was his mother. He had not the heart to disregard the silent tear that trembled neath her dark lashes when he would wish to go, so he tried to be content. He could not, however, drive his favorite project from his mind, but kept it alive, by modeling little ships, which he would sail upon the silver stream that skirted his garden.

When Joe had nearly attained his fifteenth birthday, a fine opportunity offered for him to go on a

THE OCEAN.

long cruise. An old captain, whose family lived in the same village, offered to take Joe under his especial charge, while his mother should make her home with his family until their return. After much hesitation she consented, and Joe, full of hope, donned the blue shirt and tarpaulin with a light heart, determining that, now he was started upon the world, he would make a fortune.

He was perfectly bewildered when he arrived at the great bustling city of New York, never having been so far away from home before. He had not much time to look around, for the day after his arrival the ship sailed. He was at first terribly seasick ; but a few weeks made an old sailor of him. He was charmed with the ocean and a sailor's life. He soon learned to climb the shrouds, with the best of them. They had been out about six months, when they encountered a violent storm, which made Joe, for the first time, regret that he had left home. Then, it was not his own imminent danger, but the thought of his mother, and what would become of her if he should die. Alone in the world, without a tie, the blow might be fatal. Such thoughts as these vibrated to his very soul, and awakened regrets that could not be stilled ; while the storm raged, threatening every moment to dash the frail bark to atoms, giving all her crew a watery grave among the coral depths of ocean.

God, in his providence, saw fit to order it other-

wise. The winds lulled, the dark clouds burst.
asunder, showing to the faithful sailors their silver
linings ; while the great bow of promise spanned the
heavens.

A STORM AT SEA.

After an absence of three years, the beardless boy
returned to the home of his childhood, so much altered that his own mother scarce recognized him.

How had time passed with her? Her grief was more subdued, and her step had regained a portion of its former elasticity. Each was pleased with the changes time had wrought in the other. The grateful mother hoped that her darling son would be tired of his wanderings, and spend the remainder of his life with her. But in this she was disappointed. No persuasions could keep him at home. He was born for a sailor, and a sailor he would be for life.

The next voyage he held a higher station, and the next, and so on, until he was enabled to buy a

THE OCEAN.

small craft, and be her captain. From that, he went on until, at this time, he is one of the greatest captains living, and has attained the title of Commodore.    His desire to become rich and great, through great perseverance, has been more than realized.    He is not only a millionaire, but is the owner of vessels of every description, from the gigantic steamer that plows the waves with fearful rapidity, to the little coaster, whose white sails spread to every breeze, and which is wafted along by the breath of heaven.

So you see, my little friends, that perseverance will accomplish a great deal, and it is in the power of both rich and poor to attain greatness.    Devote all your energies to one object, and success will surely follow.

THE STRANDED SHIP.

## AN EXQUISITE STORY BY LAMARTINE.

IN the tribe of Neggdah, there was a horse, whose fame was spread far and near, and a Bedouin of another tribe, by name Daher, desired extremely to possess it. Having offered in vain for it his camels and his whole wealth, he hit at length upon the following device, by which he hoped to gain the object of his desire. He resolved to stain his face with the juice of an herb, to clothe himself in rags, to tie his legs and neck together, so as to appear like a lame beggar. Thus equipped, he went to wait for Nabor, the owner of the horse, who he knew was to pass that way. When he saw Nabor approaching on his beautiful steed, he cried out in a weak voice, "I am a poor stranger, for three days I have been unable to move from this spot to seek for food. I am dying, help me and heaven will reward you." The Bedouin kindly offered to take him on his horse and carry him home ; but the rogue replied, "I cannot rise ; I have no strength left." Nabor, touched with pity, dismounted, led his horse to the spot ; and with great difficulty, set the seeming beggar on his back. But no sooner did Daher feel himself in the saddle, than he set spurs to the horse and galloped off, calling out as he did so, "It is I, Daher. I have got the horse and am off with it." Nabor called after him to stop and listen. Certain of not

AN EXQUISITE STORY BY LAMARTINE.

being pursued, he turned and halted at a short distance from Nabor, who was armed with a spear.
"You have taken my horse," said the latter.
"Since heaven has willed it, I wish you joy of it ;
but I do conjure you never to tell any one how you
obtained it." "And why not ?" said Daher. "Because," said the noble Arab, "another man might
be really ill, and men would fear to help him. You
would be the cause of many refusing to perform an
act of charity, for fear of being duped as I have
been." Struck with shame at these words, Daher
was silent for a moment, then springing from the
horse, returned it to its owner embracing him.
Nabor made him accompany him to his tent, where
they spent a few days together, and became fast
friends for life.

## WOLSEY BRIDGE; OR, THE BOY BACHELOR.

ON the south side of the ancient passage leading
from the street to the churchyard of St. Nicholas, was formerly situated the commodious house

of Thomas Wolsey, a substantial butcher and grazier, of the town of Ipswich, in the sixteenth century.

This Thomas Wolsey was one of those persons with whom the acquisition of wealth appears to be the sole purpose of existence. It was his boast "that he had thrice trebled the patrimony he had derived from his father," from whom he had inherited his flourishing business, besides some personal property. Acting in direct contradiction to that injunction of the royal psalmist, "If riches increase, set not your heart upon them ;" his very soul appeared to dwell in his money bags, his well attended shambles, or the pleasant lowland pastures where the numerous flocks and herds grazed, the profits on which he calculated would so materially improve his store. He made no show, no figure among his fellow townsmen ; never exchanging his long blue linen gown, leathern girdle, and coarse brown hose, for any other apparel, except on a Sunday, when he wore a plain substantial suit of sad colored cloth, garnished with silver buttons, and the polished steel and huge sheath knife, which he usually wore at his side, were exchanged for a silver-hilted dagger and an antique rosary and crucifix.

Satisfied with the conviction that he was one of the wealthiest tradesmen in Ipswich, he saw no reason for exciting the envy of the poor or the ill-will of the rich, by any outward demonstrations of the fact, but continued to live in the same snug, plain

manner to which he had been accustomed in his
early days, making it the chief desire of his heart
that his only son, Thomas, should tread in his steps,
and succeed him in his prosperous and well-estab-
lished business, with the same economical habits
and an equally laudable care for the main chance.

The maternal pride of his wife, Joan, who was the
descendant of a family that could **boast of gentle**
blood, prompted the secret hope that **the** ready wit
**and** studious habits, together with the clerkly skill
and learned lore which the boy had already acquired
at the grammar school, might qualify him for something better than the greasy craft of a butcher, and
perhaps one day elevate him to the situation of port
reeve or town clerk. **But** for the boy himself, **his**
youthful ambition pointed at higher marks than the
**golden** speculations of trade or **the attainment of**
lucrative offices and civic honors in his native town.

From the first moment he entered the grammar
school, and took his place on the lowest seat there,
**he** determined to occupy the highest, and to this, in
**an** almost incredibly brief period of time, he had
rapidly ascended ; and though only just entering his
twelfth year, he was the head boy in the school, and,
in the opinion of his unlearned father, " knew more
than was good for him."

As soon, indeed, as his son Thomas had learned
to write a " fair clerkly hand, to cast accounts, and
construe a page in the Breviary," he considered his

education complete, and was desirous of saving the
expense of keeping him longer at school ; but here
he was overruled by his more liberal-minded wife
Joan, who, out of the savings of her own privy purse,
paid the quarterly sum of eight-pence to the master
of the school, for the further instruction of her hopeful boy Thomas, whose abilities she regarded as

GOING TO SCHOOL.

little less than miraculous.   Persons better qualified
than the good wife, Joan Wolsey, to judge of the
natural talents and precocious acquirements of her
son, had also spoken in high terms of his progress in
the learned languages, and predicted great things of
him.    These were personages of no less importance
than the head master of the Ipswich grammar school,

and the parish priest of St. Nicholas, the latter of whom was a frequent visitor at the hospitable messuage of master Thomas Wolsey the elder, on the ostensible business of chopping Latin with young Thomas, and correcting his Greek exercises for him ; but no doubt the spiced tankards of flowing ale, and the smoking beef-steaks, cut from the very choicest part of the ox, and temptingly cooked by the well-skilled hands of that accomplished housewife, Joan Wolsey, to reward him for his good report of her darling boy's proficiency, had some influence in drawing father Boniface thither so often.

The bishop of the diocese himself had conde-scended to bestow unqualified praise on the graceful and eloquent manner in which, when he visited the school, young Wolsey had delivered the compli-mentary Latin oration on that occasion. The good-natured prelate had even condescended to pat his curly head on the conclusion of the address, and to say, " Spoken like a cardinal, my little man !"

From that moment young Wolsey had made up his mind as to his future destiny. It was to no purpose that his father tried the alternate eloquence of entreaties, reasoning, promises and threats, to de-tach him from his engrossing studies, and induce him to turn his attention to the lucrative business of a butcher and grazier. The idea of such servilely earned pelf was revolting to the excited imagination of the youthful student, whose mind was full of classic imagery, and intent on the attainment of academic honors, the steps by which he projected to ascend to the more elevated objects of his ambition.

The church was, in those days, the only avenue through which talented persons of obscure birth might hope to arrive at greatness, and young Wolsey replied to all his father's exordiums urging him to attend to the cattle market, the slaughter house, or the shambles, by announcing his intention of becoming an ecclesiastic.

The flush of anger with which this unwelcome declaration had clouded the brow of the elder Wolsey was perfectly perceptible when he returned home after the fatigues of the day to take his evening meal, which his wife, Joan, was busily engaged in preparing for him over the fire with her own hands.

" I knew how it would turn out all along of your folly, mistress, in keeping the boy loitering away his time, and learning all manner of evil habits at the grammar school, when he ought to have been bound apprentice to me, and learning our honest craft, for the last two years," muttered the malcontent butcher, throwing himself into his large arm-chair, lined with sheep-skins.

" What a coil the woman keeps up with her frying pan," continued he peevishly, on perceiving that the discreet Joan appeared disposed to drown the ebullitions of his wrath in the hissing and bubbling of the fat in her pan, as she artfully redoubled her assiduity in shaking it over the blazing hearth.

"Why, Joan," he pursued, "one cannot hear oneself speak for the noise you make."

"The noise is all of your own making, I trow, master," replied Joan, continuing to stir her hissing, sputtering pan briskly as she spoke.

"I say, leave off that frizzling with the fat in that odious pan," vociferated he.

"So I will, master, if you wish to have burnt collops for your supper to-night," replied Joan meekly.

"I don't care whether I have any supper at all," replied the butcher testily ; "I am vexed, mistress."

"Good lack ! what should happen to vex you, master !" responded his wife. "I am sure the world always seems to wag the way you'd have it go ; but losses and crosses in business will chance even to the most prosperous, at times. Is one of your fat beasts dead ?"

"No !"

"Some of your best sheep been stolen ?"

"No !"

"Mayhap then, some customer, whom you have suffered to run up a long score, is either dead or bankrupt ?"

"Worse than that, mistress."

"I prythee, good Thomas, let me hear the truth at once," exclaimed the startled Joan, upsetting the frying pan into the fire in her alarm. "The misfortune must be great that hath befallen you, if it be reckoned by you worse than the loss of money."

" Why, mistress, do not you reckon the perverse inclinations of one's own flesh and blood a more serious calamity than loss of substance?"

" Aye, master; but that is a trial we have never had the sorrow of knowing since our only son, Thomas, albeit I say it who ought not, is the most dutiful, diligent, and loving lad, that ever blessed a parent's heart," said the fond mother, melting into tears of tenderness as she spoke.

" Hold thy peace, dame," cried the indignant husband, darting a look of angry reproach on the offending youth, who had been comfortably reposing himself on an oaken settle by the fireside, reading Virgil's Eneid by the light of the blazing embers, during the whole of the discussion, without concerning himself about any thing, save to preserve the beloved volume from being sprayed by the fat which the frying-pan, in falling, had scattered in all directions. " That lad, on whom you bestow such foolish commendations," pursued old Wolsey; " that lad, whatever might have been his former virtuous inclinations, has now disappointed all my hopes, for he hath turned an errant scape-grace, and refuseth to become a butcher, though the shambles he would inherit from me are the largest, the most commodious, and the best frequented with ready-penny customers, of any on the market hill. Moreover, it is a business in which his grandfather got money, and I, following in his good steps, with still better

success, have become—I scorn to boast, but the
truth may be spoken without blame—one of the
wealthiest tradesmen in the borough."

"Then the less need, my master, of enforcing
such a clever lad as our Thomas to follow a craft
which is so unsuitable for a scholar," observed Joan.

"There," groaned the butcher, "was the folly of
making him one, which hath been the means of
teaching him to slight the main chance, and to turn
his head with pagan poesies or monkish lore. Would
you believe it, mistress Joan,—he hath had the
audacity to profess his desire of becoming a student
at the university of Oxenford !"

"And why should he not, master Wolsey, since
he promiseth to become a learned clerk ?" asked the
proud mother.

"To what purpose should he go thither ?" said
the father.

"Marry, master, to increase his learning, and to
put him in the way of becoming a great man,"
responded mistress Joan.

"A great man, forsooth !" echoed her husband
contemptuously ; "who ever heard of a butcher's
son becoming a person of distinction ?"

"I have heard, sir," said young Wolsey, closing
his book eagerly ; "I have heard of a destitute
swineherd becoming a pope."

"Indeed !" ejaculated his father with an air of
incredulity.

" Yes, sir, it was Nicholas Brekespeare, afterwards Pope Adrian the Fourth, the only Englishman who ever filled the papal chair, but perhaps not the last whom learning, combined with persevering enterprise, may conduct to that eminence."

" Ho ! ho ! ho !" cried the butcher, bursting into a loud laugh ; " I wist not of the high mark at which your ambition aimeth, son Thomas ! Well, if enabling you to become a servitor in Magdalen College will advance your holiness one step towards the possession of St. Peter's keys, I will not withhold my assistance and my blessing, though much I doubt whether it will carry thee into the Vatican, or whatever you call it, of which you and Father Boniface are always talking."

" And what if it do not carry him quite so far, master," interposed Joan, "didst thou never hear of the proverb, He who reacheth after a gown of cloth of gold, shall scarcely fail of getting one of the sleeves ?"

" Ay, mother !" cried young Wolsey ; " and when I am a cardinal, my father will thank you for the parable."

" Ah ! if I ever live to see that day, son Thomas !" observed the butcher.

" Why should you doubt it, master ?" asked mistress Joan.

" Because, wife, it is easy to talk of dignities and honors, but to obtain them would be attended with difficulties, which I doubt our simple son, **Thomas,** will find insurmountable."

"I shall, at least, lose nothing in making the attempt," observed young Wolsey.

"There **is** your mistake, boy ; you will **lose** something **very** considerable," replied his father.

"Dear father, what can that be for which the learning I shall acquire **will not make** me ample amends ?"

"The most flourishing butchery in Ipswich, simpleton ! which, if once lost through your inconsiderate folly, you may study till doomsday, and acquire all the learning in popedom and heathenesse into the bargain, without being able to re-establish it in its present prosperity," returned the mortified father with **a** groan.

**A smile which the** younger **Wolsey strove in vain to repress, played over his features at these words.**

"**Ay, scorn and** slight the substantial good that is within your reach for the sake of the vain shadow which is beyond your power to obtain, Thomas Wolsey," said his father with great bitterness.

"My dear father, you know little of the powers of the human mind, or of the mighty things which its energies, when once roused, and directed towards one object may effect."

"I tell you, Thomas, that the end you propose **is** *impossible.*"

"Sir," replied young Wolsey, "I have blotted *that word* out of **MY** dictionary."

"I like your spirit, young man," said his father, "albeit it savoreth a little of presumption."

"That remains to be proved," said his son, "and I am quite ready that my earnestness should be tried by any test you may be inclined to demand."

"I shall hold you to your word," replied his father, "and condition, that if you take up your bachelor's degree within four years of your entering Magdalen College, then shall you proceed in the course of life on which you are so determinately bent ; but if you fail in doing this, then shall you return to my house, and submit your future destiny to my disposal."

"If I take it not up within two years of my entering the college, barring accidents of sickness or death, then strip me of the learned stole of a clerk of Oxenford, and chain me to your girdle as a butcher's slave for life," replied the youth with heightened color.

"Thou hast pledged thyself to that which thou canst not perform, son Thomas," replied his father. "Who ever heard of a boy of fourteen taking up a bachelor's degree at Oxenford ?"

"Thou shalt hear of one anon, mine honored father," said young Wolsey.

"I will engage that thy mother shall have the finest baron of beef in my shambles to roast for dinner on the day on which I hear that news," rejoined his father.

"See that you keep my father to his promise,

mother," said the youth, "for I shall travel night
and day, in hopes of being the first to communicate
the intelligence, or at any rate, to arrive in time to
come in for a slice of the beef while it be hot."

The important object being now accomplished of
obtaining the consent of the elder Wolsey to his
son's entering the university of Oxford, the lad
commenced his journey on the following day for that

ancient seat of learning. He was on foot, for the
sturdy butcher, his father, though well able to send
him thither on a stout pack-horse, attended by one
of his own men, was determined to afford no facilities
for an enterprise to which he had so little relish.

The loving care of mistress Joan Wolsey had supplied the youthful candidate for scarlet stockings
and cardinal's hat with a few silver groats for his
expenses on the road, and a needful stock of linen
and other necessaries, which he carried in a leathern
wallet in one hand, and in the other a stout oaken
staff; but that which young Wolsey considered
more precious than either money or apparel, was a
letter of recommendation from the head master of
the Ipswich grammar school to the master of Magdalen College.

This credential obtained for its lonely and friend-
less bearer that attention which his juvenile appearance, diminutive stature, and his coarse and travel-
soiled attire, would most probably have failed of
attracting.

Having passed his examination with great credit
to himself, he was admitted as a servitor of Magdalen College. In this novel situation young Wolsey had some difficulties, and not a few hardships
and privations, to contend with; but these, when
weighed against the mighty object which engrossed
all his thoughts, were as dust in the balance, and
the only effect they had was to increase his perse-

vering diligence. **At the** end of the first term he had made a progress which astonished his masters and fellow students. Before the two years had expired within which the lad had pledged himself **to take up a** degree, an attempt which his father with reason judged unattainable by a person of his tender age, the good-wife Joan Wolsey, in great haste, entered the shambles, where her husband was preparing to put an uncommonly fine baron of beef into the basket of a nobleman's servant, and laying hands upon it, exclaimed, "Why, Thomas Wolsey, what are you about to do with that meat?"

"To send it to the house of my lord, according to order, to be sure, mistress," replied the butcher, with a look of surprise.

"**An it had been ordered by King** Henry himself, he should not **have it** to-day," said Mistress Joan.

"Is your wife delirit, master Wolsey?" asked the servant.

"One would suppose so by her wild words," said the astonished butcher, who knew not what to think of the behavior of his usually discreet sponse.

"If I be, master, it is with joy," replied **Joan** Wolsey; "but the truth is, I came hither to claim the finest baron of beef in the shambles, which you said I should roast for dinner on the day on which you heard the news of our son, Thomas Wolsey, taking up a bachelor's degree at Oxenford."

"And who brought you the intelligence, mistress?" demanded her husband.

"A joyful messenger, my good man, for it was the boy himself, blessings on him ! dressed in his bachelor's gown, and bearing the certificate of his admission as a fellow of Magdalen College."

"Humphrey !" cried the delighted father, turning to his head-man, " take that baron of beef home to my house, and help thy mistress to split it, and put it down to the fire, that my boy bachelor may dine off the best joint in my shambles ; and do you, master Ralph," added he, turning to his lordship's servant, " make my duty to my lord, and ask him, if he will be pleased to put up with rump or ribs to-day, since the baron of beef, for which his house-keeper hath sent, was bespoken nearly two years before his order came, and my good dame hath come to claim my pledge in earnest."

" Which my lord is too strict an observer of his own word to wish you to forfeit on his account, I am sure, master Wolsey," said Ralph : "and when I explain the pleasant cause for which you have made bold to disappoint his lordship of his favorite dish to-day, he, who is himself a scholar and a patron of learning withal, will hold you excused."

This day being a holiday, the head master of the Ipswich grammar school, several of young Wolsey's chosen friends among the scholars, and the good-humored curate of St. Nicholas, were invited to par-

take of the baron of beef which the young bachelor
had so honorably earned, and which Mrs. Joan Wolsey cooked in her most approved style, to the great
satisfaction of her husband and the guests.

This was one of the long vacations, but no season
of idleness to young Wolsey, whose unremitting ap-
plication to study impaired his appetite, and rendered him languid and feverish, which his anxious
mother perceiving, and feeling some alarm lest his
incessant mental toil might injure his naturally feeble constitution, she communicated her uneasiness
to her husband, and asked him if he could not con-
trive some little pleasant employment for him, which
would have the effect of diverting him for a few
days from his sedentary occupations.

"Ay, ay, dame," replied old Wolsey, "I have a
choice bit of pastime for the boy ; he shall go with
Humphrey and Peter and Miles to buy beeves off
the Southwold and Reydon commons and marshes."

"That would do well enough, master, if the lad
were any judge of cattle, which I fear, with all his
college learning, he is not," responded mistress
Joan.

"You may well say that, mistress," rejoined the
butcher, "for, though he hath been born, bred, and
nourished in the midst of such matters, and he is
observant enough in other things, yet I would answer for it, he knoweth not the difference between
a fat beast and a lean one, a Scot or a home-bred,

yea scarcely between a long horn or a short ; and
were I to send him on this business of mine without
my shrewd foreman, Humphrey, to instruct *his* ignorance and detect the knavery of the sellers, he
would bring me home pretty bargains of beasts

against the Easter festivals.    Why these fat monks
of Reydon, who are far better skilled in grazing for
the Ipswich and Yarmouth markets than in their
church Latin, would be sure to palm their old worn-
out mortuary cows upon him for fine young heifers,
and make him pay the price of three-year old steers

for their broken-down yoke oxen that had plowed the convent lands for the last ten years. But, as I said before, Humphrey shall go with him, who is used to their tricks of old, and will bid them half their asking price at a word, which our Thomas would be ashamed of doing to men of their cloth were he left to himself, so he shall only have the pleasant part of the business, to wit, listening to the chaffering, and paying down the money when the price is agreed upon by those who are wiser in such matters than himself."

"And how do you propose for him to perform the journey, master, for the places whereof you speak are many miles distant?" said Joan.

"Under forty miles, wife, which will be no great stretch for Miles and Peter (who are to drive the cattle) to walk; as for Thomas, he shall ride my gray mare, and Humphrey can take the black nag, and give Miles and Peter a lift behind him by turns, which will ease their legs, and make it a pleasant journey for them all. Ah! that part of Suffolk is a fine grazing country to travel through. I am sure I shall envy Thomas the prospect of so many herds and flocks as he will see on those upland meads and salt-marshes; but he will think more of chopping Latin with the monks of Blitheborough, and looking over their old musty books and records, which could never give a hungry man his dinner, than of all the sensible sights he might see by the way."

" Every one to his vocation, master," replied Joan
Wolsey ; " yours is to feed the bodies, and my
Thomas' will be to nourish the minds of men with
a more enduring food than that which you-have it
in your power to provide."

"Gramercy, mistress !" said the butcher, with a
grin ; " one would think he had been feasting you
on some of his improving diet, for you begin to
discourse like a doctor."

The next day by peep of dawn, the quartette set
forth from St. Nicholas' passage on their expedition,
on which no one reckoned more than young Wolsey,
who wearing his college cap and gown, the latter of
which was tucked up round his waist, lest its long
full skirts should impede his horsemanship, was
mounted on his father's easy-pacing gray mare.
For the convenience of riding he was accommodated
with a pair of the old man's boots, which drew up
far above his knees, and were wide enough to admit
three pair of legs like the stripling's slender limbs.
He rode cautiously at the head of the cavalcade,
taking care to keep close to Humphrey, who jogged
along very comfortably on the black nag, whose
mettle, if ever it had possessed any, was tamed by
the wear and tear of fifteen years of service in the
butcher's cart.

Miles and Peter trudged steadily along with their
quarter staffs in their hands, relying on their own
excellent pedestrianism to reach the ultimate place

of their destination almost as soon as the horsemen
of the party, whose steeds they knew would be
sorely jaded before they reached St. Peter's, Wangford, where their master had directed them to crave
lodging for the night of the monks of Clugni, who
there occupied a cell dependent on the monastery
of Thetford, which also was the parent house of the
cell at Reydon.

The two saucy knaves occasionally exchanged sly
glances, and cracked dry jokes on the unsuitable
array and cautious riding of the young Oxford
student, their master's son, and the steady jog trot
of Humphrey, who rode quite at his ease on a soft
sheepskin which supplied the place of a saddle, by
being tightly buckled with a broad leathern strap
under the belly of the black nag, whose quiet temper allowed her to be ridden safely without stirrups.

The sun rose brightly in a soft April sky by the
time they reached Woodbridge. Young Wolsey
had now become familiar with the paces of the gray
mare, and the excitement of the exercise, the beauty
of the morning, the invigorating freshness of the air,
and lovely succession of new and agreeable objects,
contributing to raise his spirits, he soon began to
assume a little more of the cavalier, and occasionally
used the whip and the spurs, in defiance of all
Humphrey's prudential cautions. Nature had well
qualified the youthful student, both in form and
agility, to play the graceful horseman, and before

they arrived at Wickham Market, the skill and boldness with which he managed his steed was a matter of surprise to the whole party.

At this little town they stopped, and refreshed both men and beasts with a substantial breakfast, and then set forward on their journey with renewed spirits. Young Wolsey, who had a purpose of his own to answer, put his father's mare to her speed, and soon left the pedestrian Peter, and the hapless nag with its double burden, of Humphrey and Miles, far in the rear, regardless of their shouts of "Fair play, master Thomas! fair play!" and "Alack, alack, sir, have a care of our good master's mare!"

But the stripling, who liked not the repeated hints which Humphrey had given him of the propriety and expediency, to say nothing of the kindness, of giving poor Peter a lift behind him, now they were clear of the houses, was determined to ride forward, not wishing the bachelor's cap and gown to appear in such close fellowship with the butcher's blue and greasy buff of his father's men. Besides, he greatly desired, instead of keeping the jog-trot pace that suited their convenience, to gain an hour or two to spend with the monks of the Holyrood at Blitheborough, and to examine the antiquities, architecture, and localities of that ancient and interesting place, through which the route chalked out for him by his father lay; but the elder Wolsey had strictly charged Humphrey in his hear-

ing, " not to permit his young master to delay their
journey, by wasting his time and theirs in prating
Lating gibberish with the black locust of Blitheborough," (as he irreverently styled those worthy
anchorites,) "especially as he did not want to deal
with them for sheep, the last he had bought off their
walks having proved a very bad bargain."

Now young Wolsey, when he heard this caution,
secretely resolved to arrange matters so as to enjoy
the conference with the monks without either infrin-
ging his father's directions, or being pestered with
the company of his blue-frocked retainers. So he
prest his mare on, and though, as well as her, sorely
wearied with the unwonted number of miles he had
traversed, his youthful spirits carried him forward
with unabated energy, till, on descending the last
hill after crossing the extensive track of purple heath,
known by the name of Blitheborough Sheep-walks,
that most stately structure, the church of the Holy
Trinity, rose before him in all the magnificence of
the monastic ages of its glory, in the elaborate rich-
ness of the florid gothic architecture, untouched by
time and unimpaired by accident, with the bright
sunbeams playing and flashing on the many-colored
stains of its wide and lofty windows.

Young Wolsey checked his horse, and gazed upon
this noble edifice with the enthusiasm natural to
the future founder of colleges and gothic buildings ;
then slowly, and looking often backwards, he pro-

ceeded to the cell and chapel of the **Holyrood,** which
indeed was so contiguous to the spot **that he was**
able still to enjoy a close view of the new church, **as**
it was then called, while he partook of the good
cheer which the hospitable fraternity produced for
his refreshment, and **to** which the hungry stripling
did ample justice.

**As** the bells were chiming for vespers, monastic
etiquette compelled him to accompany the monks
to their pretty chapel ; and when the evening service
was concluded, **the** friendly monks gratified their
**visitor with an interior** view of **the** church **of** the
Holy Trinity, and pointed out **to him its rich car-**
vings, screens, trellises, and magnificently **sculp-**
tured and emblazoned roof.

Young Wolsey had been too deeply engaged in
the contemplation of these interesting localities to
embrace the opportunity of displaying his own
learning to the friendly monks, who had treated him
with the respect which his natural talents and early
**acquirements** were well calculated to inspire, and
pressingly invited him to sojourn with them during
**the** rest of the evening, and pass the night **in** their
dormitory ; but the importunities of Humphrey
(who, with Peter and Miles, had arrived while he
was at Vespers, and having refreshed them**selves**
and the black nag, were now clamorous to proceed)
prevailing over his desire of accepting an invitation
so agreeable to his own inclinations, he **took a lov-**

ing farewell of the hospitable fraternity, promising
to find some way of gratifying his wish of passing a
few hours with them on his return. Then mounting the gray mare, he rode forward at a gentle pace
with his weary and somewhat malcontent companions, who scrupled not to reproach him for the want
of good fellowship he had displayed in deserting
their company. Nor did Humphrey fail to exert
the privilege of an old and trusted servant, by rating
his young master soundly for having over-heated
the gray mare on a long journey, besides incurring
much peril of accidents both to himself and that
valuable animal, on account of his being an inexperienced rider, and quite unacquainted with the
road.

The young student who was of course rather impatient of these rebukes, which he considered very
derogatory to the dignity of a bachelor of Oxford to
receive from butchers and cattle drovers, endeavored
to escape from them by a repetition of his offence,
namely, outriding the party ; but that was no longer in his power, for he had fairly knocked up the
gray mare so that she was unable to compete with
the shabby nag on which Humphrey rode, and the
only alternative left him was to listen meekly, or to
turn a deaf ear, to the reproaches that assailed him
right and left, and amuse himself with his own re-
flections, or in contemplating the charms of the
varied landscape before him, when, on ascending the

gentle hill leading from Blitheburgh, he found himself among the rich woods and cowslipped meads of
Henham, whose castellated hall, then the residence
of the Brandons, rose in all its gothic grandeur over
grove and vale, as the crowning object of the prospect, but was soon after hidden behind the inter-
vening screen of deep embowering shades, which
were then almost impervious to the light of day, and
converted the advancing gloom of evening into early
night.   No sooner was the party involved in this
obscurity, than the offended trio, Humphrey, Miles,
and Peter, united their voices in a universal chorus
of grumbling at their detention at Blitheburgh, declaring they were benighted, and should in all
probability be robbed of the sum entrusted to them
for the purchase of the cattle.

The welcome sound of the curfew bell of St.
Peter's, Wangford, however, soon informed them
that their apprehensions were groundless, and put
them into better humor, by advertising them that
they were not more than a mile distant from the
place of their destination ; and presently, after
emerging from beneath the sombre shadows of Henham's oaken glades, they found themselves once
more in day-light, and in the immediate vicinity of
the pretty village of Wangford, which, with its
picturesque monastery and chapel of St. Peter's,
crowning a gentle eminence, lay full before them.

The pastoral rivulet of the Wang, from which

the name of this hamlet is derived, was soon forded by the weary travelers, who, proceeding to the little convent, obtained without difficulty food and shelter for the night. The next morning, as soon as matins were over, which service they of course considered themselves bound to attend, they set forward on their short journey to the neighboring monastery of Reydon.

Leaving its green bowery labyrinth of sylvan lanes, its antique hall and park, its aboriginal forest and the gray spire of its venerable church, and all that was pleasing and attractive in the landscape of the Reydon, or the red hill (which its Saxon name signifies,) to the left, Humphrey guided the party through a narrow, wet, and incommodious road, to a mean conventual building, situated at the most desolate extremity of the parish, among the salt marshes.

If Wolsey had expected to find learning, piety, or hospitality among this fraternity, he was certainly much dissapointed ; for a set of more illiterate and narrow-minded men than these Reydon monks were never congregated together. Far from expressing the least interest in the acquirements of their accomplished young guest, they received the intelligence of his proficiency in the learned languages with dismay, and appeared far better pleased with the conversation of Humphrey, Peter and Miles, which indeed was more in unison with their tastes than that

of the scholastic Wolsey, whom they entertained
with long dissertations, not on the fathers or the
classics, but on the most profitable breeds of cattle,
and the most approved modes of fatting swine, in
all which matters they were very fluent, and appeared to consider it passing strange that a butcher's son
possessed so little knowledge on such interesting
topics. They also discussed the best methods of
curing white bacon, as the fat of pickled pork is
called in that part of Suffolk. On this delectable
article Wolsey and his party had the felicity of sup-
ping that evening, which he afterwards declared was
the dullest he ever spent in the whole course of his
life.

The next morning the fraternity proceeded with
their guests to the marshes where their cattle fed,
where a long and animated discussion took place
between Humphrey and the superior of the convent
respecting the price, the merits, and defects of the
beasts which Humphrey deemed most worthy of his
attention, in which so much time was wasted that
the dinner bell rang before they had settled the price
of so much as one bullock.

At this meal they were again regaled with white
bacon, which appeared a standing dish in this convent, for it was produced at supper, breakfast, and
dinner ; at the latter, indeed, there was the addition
of a huge dish of hard dumplings, with which they
devoured a quantity of pork-dripping by way of sauce.

The morning had been fine but showery, in the afternoon a heavy rain set in, which rendered it impossible either to visit the cattle-marshes again, or to proceed homewards, which young Wolsey recommended his father's men to do, on the conviction of the impossibility of ever concluding a bargain with these frocked and cowled dealers in cattle and feeders of swine.

The rain, however, continued without intermission, and the malcontent student was compelled to remain where he was till the "plague of water," as he called this unwelcome down-pouring, should abate.

The following morning proving fine, they again proceeded to the marshes in hope of striking a bargain, which was at length concluded ; but not till after a delay that appeared to the impatient Wolsey almost interminable, which time he employed, not in listening to the altercations of the buyer and sellers of the bullocks ; but in strolling through the marshes and making observations, till he obtained a view of Blitheburgh on the line of country that intervened, across which he persuaded himself a much shorter cut to that village might be made than by following the usual road through Wangford. Just as he had come to the resolution of attempting that route, the convent bell rang for dinner, and summoned him to a sixth meal of white bacon, of which the monks ate with as keen an appetite as if it had

been the first time they ever partook of that savory
fare, of which Wolsey was by this time almost as
weary as of the company of the founders of the entertainment.

The bullocks, twelve in number, were now driven
into the convent yard, and Humphrey called upon
his young master to pay down the price for which
he and the monks had agreed, at the average sum of
one pound ten shillings a head, which he pronounced
an unconscionable sum with a sly wink of intelligence at the Oxford student, by which he gave the
youth, who was about to take his words literally, to
understand that he was well satisfied with the bargain. In fact, the Reydon monks, shrewd and ex-
acting as they were, had met with more than their
match in the calculating, experienced Humphrey,
who, without making a boast of his wisdom in this
way, knew how to judge of the weight of a living ox
almost to an odd pound. Till the business was
concluded, the money paid, and the receipt given,
he had forborne to taste of the convent mead or ale,
though both had been pressed upon him with an
earnestness passing the bounds either of politeness
or hospitality by the cunning monks, who hoped to
overcome Humphrey's cool, clear judgment and
caution, by means of the merry brown bowl ; but
now all fear of being overreached in his bargain in
consequence of such an indulgence was at an end,
Humphrey, in spite of all his young master's ex-

postulations, demanded the lately-rejected beverage, of which he, with Miles and Peter, drank pretty freely, though not perhaps so much as they would have done had the cloistered cattle-dealers been willing to produce more, which they were always sparing in doing after a bargain had been definitely struck.

The draughts which the trio had swallowed had had, however, the effect of putting them all into such high good humor, that when Wolsey, on mounting, proposed to them his plan of changing the roundabout route through Wangford, for a straight cut across the marshes to Blitheburgh, they offered no objection, for even the prudent Humphrey was desirous of adopting any expedient by which they might make up for the time they had lost in drinking the convent ale after the business was transacted.

The monks assured them the project was feasible, since the branch of the Blithe which separated Henham and Reydon was fordable, and they would save a considerable distance by crosing the river, but their hospitality did not extend to the civility of sending one of their swine-herds or goose-boys to point out the precise spot at which the attempt might be made without danger to passengers. The stream was much swollen in consequence of the late heavy rains; Humphrey and the drovers paused on the rushy bank, each prudently declining to be the first to try the ford. Wolsey, who was piqued at their doubts of his assurance " that it was safe ! perfectly safe !" though he would rather have had one of the others show a demonstrable proof that there was no danger, urged his reluctant mare forward.

" Hold, master Thomas, hold ! for the love of St. Margaret," cried Humphrey, who was suddenly sobered by the sight of his young master's peril, and the recollection that the stream was deep and muddy·

" Now this St. Margaret was a saint for whom Wolsey had neither love nor reverence ; so, without heeding the adjuration so pathetically addressed to him in her name, he boldly plunged into the dark and swollen waters of the dangerous ford. He was, as we have seen, an inexperienced rider on dry land, but a more skillful horseman than the stripling student would have found it a difficult matter to retain his seat and guide the terrified animal, who presently lost her footing, and began to plunge and kick in the muddy slippery ooze of which the bed of the Blithe and its dependent streams are composed, and which having recently been violently disturbed by the heavy rains, was in a state of complete ferment and liquefaction.

Wolsey, though encumbered with his bachelor's gown, which he had not this time taken the precautionary measure of tucking up and fastening to his girdle, courageously maintained his seat till the mare, exhausted with her violent efforts, sunk, and left him floating on the stream. He was an expert swimmer in the clear calm Orwell, or the pastoral Gipping, his native streams, but scarcely a fish that had been used to the fresh sparkling element of such rivers as these, could have steered its course in the dark vortex of brackish mud in which poor Wolsey was immersed.

Peter and Miles stood aghast at the accident, uttering doleful cries for help, without venturing to make a single effort to save the almost exhausted youth. Humphrey, the faithful Humphrey, at the first alarm had dismounted from the nag, and was preparing to plunge into the stream to save his master's son or perish in the attempt, when one of Sir Richard Brandon's wood-rangers, who had seen the accident and hastened to the spot, reached the end of the long pole he had been using in leaping the marsh ditches, to the youth, by which assistance, the stream being narrow at that place, he was enabled, though not without some difficulty, to gain the opposite bank, from which, as soon as he had cleared his eyes and mouth of the salt, bitter, and unsavory ooze he had been compelled to swallow, he called out in an accent of distress to Humphrey, " O, Humphrey, Humphrey ! what shall we say to my father about the gray mare ?"

" St. Margaret take the mare !" sobbed Humphrey, who appeared to consider this patroness as somehow chargeable with the mishap ; " don't talk of her, my dear boy, when she had nearly been the death of you. Howsomdever, master Thomas, you must never undertake to lead those who are wiser than yourself short cuts any more. I hope you have had enough of this precious ford, that was to take you such a near way to Blitheburgh."

"Why so it will, you simple fellow," said Wolsey laughing, and wiping the mud from his face ; "do not you see the beautiful church over those marshes, almost at my elbow ?  I shall bestir myself to get there as fast as I can, now I *am* over the water, that I may get dry clothes, a good supper, and some pleasant chat with the worthy monks of the Holy Rood, which will console me for the drenching I have got."

"Alack, alack ! master Thomas ! what is to become of us and the bullocks ?" howled Miles and Peter from the opposite bank.

"You may come over the river to me, an you like," responded Wolsey from the other side.

"We durst not do that for our lives," cried the trembling drovers.

"Then turn yourselves and the bullocks about, and find the road to Wangford as well as ye can : Humphrey knows the country, and he will guide ye to get to Blitheburgh by that roundabout way, ye poltroons, unless ye choose to stay where ye are till I am a Cardinal, when it is my intention to build a bridge over this sweet stream, to prevent other travelers from incurring the peril which I have done in endeavoring to ford such a bottomless abyss of mud."

We **will not** follow the young bachelor to Blitheburgh, **where,** doubtless, he met with agreeable entertainment, nor will the limits of our tale admit of our tracing the progressive steps by which he in **the** sequel attained to the eminence to which his ambition, even in childhood, prompted him to aspire. By keeping his attention constantly fixed on this object, he found it at last within his reach ; but was he then contented ? Let me answer this question with another—When was the desire of human greatness ever satisfied ? I refer the juvenile reader to the **history of this extraordinary man, who,** when **he had attained the coveted** rank **of Cardinal,** though **he was** burdened **with** the cares of the prime minis**ter of** England, which office he held during twenty years of Henry the Eighth's reign, was not forgetful of his promise of building a bridge over the stream which had so nearly proved fatal to himself. The name of the bridge, and the local tradition thereunto belonging, will long, I trust, exist to preserve the memory of an action **of** pure benevolence to future ages.

## TALE OF THE THREE SPINNERS.

ONCE upon a time, there was a lazy maiden, who would not spin ; and her mother might say what she pleased, yet could not persuade her to it. But at last anger and impatience overcame the mother, and she gave her a blow, at which she began to weep loudly. Just at that time, the queen rode by in a carriage, and stopping when she heard the weeping, asked the mother why she was beating her daughter so hard, that one without could plainly hear the blows. But the woman was ashamed to disclose the indolence of her daughter, and said : " I cannot prevent her from spinning ; she will spin forever and ever ; and I am so poor, that I cannot procure the flax." Then the queen said : " There is nothing that I delight in so much as spinning, and am never so happy as when I see the wheel whirl round ; permit me to take your daughter to my castle, where I have plenty of flax ; she shall then spin as much as she pleases." The mother consented with all her heart, and the queen took away the maiden. When they had come to the castle, she conducted her up to three chambers, which were full of the finest flax from top to bottom. " Now spin me this flax," said she, " and when you have got it done, you shall have my eldest son for a husband ; though you are poor, yet I won't mind

TALE OF THE THREE SPINNERS.

that ; your unwearied industry is dowry enough."
The maiden was inwardly frightened, as she knew
that she could not spin the flax even if she lived to
the age of three hundred, and sat at it all day from
morning till night.    As she was now alone, she began to weep, and sat so three days without stirring.
On the third day, the queen came, and when she
saw that she had done nothing, she was surprised ;
but the maiden excused herself by saying that she
had not yet been able to commence her work, in
consequence of her great sadness occasioned by her
removal from her mother.    The queen put up with
it, but said, on going away : "In the morning you
must begin to work for me "

Now when the maiden was all alone, she was at a
perfect loss to know what to do, and went sadly up
to the window.    There she saw three women coming
toward her, of whom the first had a huge flat foot ;
the second had a monstrous under-lip, that hung
down over her chin, and the third had a great
thumb.  As she remained there sorrowfully, they
stood still, cried out, and asked the maiden what
ailed her.  When she complained of her trouble,
they offered their assistance to her, and said : "If
you will invite us to the wedding-feast, and not be
ashamed to call us your aunts, and moreover give us
a seat at your table, we will spin your flax for you,
and that, too, in a very short time."  "With all my
heart," she replied ; " only come in and set to work

quickly.' Then she let the three strange women in, and concealed them in the first chamber, where they might sit down and begin their spinning. One drew out the thread and trod the wheel; the second knit it; the third twisted it, and beat with her fingers on the table, and as often as she beat, there fell to the floor a skein of yarn, which was spun in the finest manner. She concealed the spinners from the queen, and showed to her as often as she came, the quantity of yarn spun, so that she received continual praise. When the first chamber was emptied, they came to the second, and finally to the third, and that was at last finished. Now the three women took leave, and said to the maiden: " Do not forget what you have promised us—it will be your fortune."

When the maiden pointed out to the queen the empty chambers, and the great heaps of yarn, she made preparations for the wedding-feast; and the bridegroom rejoiced that he was to have so skillful and industrious a wife, and was exceedingly pleased.

"I have three aunts," said the maiden, "who have shown me a great deal of kindness; therefore I would not willingly forget them in my good fortunes; give me permission, pray, to invite them to the wedding, and seat them at the table." The queen and the bridegroom readily granted her request. When the feast began, the three spinners entered in a strange costume, and the bride said: "I am glad to see you, dear aunts." "O," said the bridegroom, "how did you come by such ugly relatives?" Then he went to the first with the

SPINNING.

huge flat foot, and said : "How did you get such a monstrous foot?" "By treading," she replied, "by treading." Then he came to the second, also, and said : "Do tell me how you got that huge under lip?" "By wetting the thread," she replied, "by wetting the thread." Then he said to the third : "How did you get your great thumb?" "By twisting the thread," she replied, "by twisting the thread." And the king's son was frightened, and said : "Then my dear bride shall never again touch a wheel." Thus she got rid of the disagreeable task of spinning flax.

## SOMEBODY NOT PLEASED WITH HIS NAME.

HERE lived, many long years ago, a man called Somebody, and there was nothing which he disliked so much as this name. "All the misfortunes I have met with in the world are entirely owing to my name," he was wont to say; "and if I could but get a rich estate by so doing, I would part with it directly; for there always must be Somebody for people to scold when they are in a bad temper—Somebody whom they can laugh at or persecute.

"There is not even a children's party where Somebody is not teased or annoyed. They are sure to make a laughing-stock of Somebody. Somebody always comes badly off, when fruit and cakes are divided; and when the children have grown up into sensible people, it is not much better. Go to a tea-party, and see if Somebody is not pulled over the coals a little, if Somebody is not blamed, or if some evil is not spoken of him.

"Is there any hard work to be done, and no one has any inclination to set about it, Somebody must do it. Is anything broken in the house, Somebody must have done it. Does **anything** come **to** light which ought to have been **kept a secret,** Somebody must **have let it** out ; **and if any** foolish prank **is set** on foot, Somebody is sure **to be** the sufferer."

And, therefore, as Somebody was exposed to so much injustice, and had to bear so much **that was** disagreeable, he took quite **a** dislike **to his** name, and determined **to give** another **to** his only child—a beautiful, lively boy—hoping that he might not experience the same annoyance. "He shall be called Nobody," said he. "He will not be much talked about, and people will leave him to himself. **No**body is safe from slanderers. **Proud people are po**lite to Nobody ; **and I have always heard** that the stingy **are generous to Nobody."**

And so Somebody's child was christened **Nobody—** a very lucky idea, as it seemed, for not long afterward dear "Nobody" was spoken of on all sides, and the child seemed in a fair way to make his fortune in the world. His father, however, did not live to see **it.** One day the funeral bell tolled, and people said, carelessly, Somebody is dead. Nobody followed the coffin ; Nobody wept very bitterly—so is it almost always when the poor and unfortunate die !

And now the child was quite alone. He **went** away from the churchyard, and along the high road without exactly knowing what would become of him. At length he came to a beautiful garden, in which fountains, stone statues, an aviary, and a tame ape were to be seen ; but before the garden was a cast-iron gate, with black rails, having a bar, fastened tightly, drawn in front.

" Who is allowed to come in here ?" asked the child, of a brisk little gardener-boy, who happened to pass by with a basketful of beautiful melons.

" Nobody," answered he, which reply gave our little boy no small delight.

Without allowing himself much time for reflection he climbed nimbly over the iron-gate rails, and jumped down, without hurting himself, into the deep white sand. Who now could be better off than he ?

Nobody might walk on the green velvet turf ; Nobody might break off a flower if he wished—at least so it was stated, in large letters, upon the boards which were erected in various parts of the garden ; so he made himself very comfortable, and laid himself down in the cool shade, under a tree, close by the splashing fountains, while he refreshed himself with a few oranges, which he had gathered as he passed through a forcing-house. " I have free entrances everywhere here," thought he ; " and all seems made for me, as it were. I will not be squeamish ; I wish I could see the kind owner of this garden, and thank him for his goodness."

When he had rested sufficiently, and had quench-ed his thirst with the beautiful juicy fruit, the child rose up once more, and wandered still farther and farther into the garden. With every step he discovered fresh beauties ; the flowers at length became less numerous, and he reached a wide, open square, in which stood a castle—not so very spacious, perhaps, but so splendid, that the poor boy's eyes, heavy with weeping, were opened quite widely to look at it.

He had never till then seen so handsome a window, or so wide a balcony. Flowers and climbing plants covered the latter, above which a canopy of purple silk was extended. And wonderingly he gazed at the elaborately carved columns which, apparently, supported the beautiful edifice. A pair of chattering parrots were swinging to and fro, in their metal rings, among the flowers, and called out with hoarse voices, " Who is there ?" " Who are you ?"

The little fellow took his cap off quickly, looking very red and frightened, and answered—" Pray forgive my having come in here ; I do not wish to disturb you, and will go away again. My name is Nobody, and I am Somebody's son."

Having modestly answered the parrots, the little boy determined upon retracing his steps, only that he first wished to know to whom this wonderful castle belonged. He next discovered at the entrance, a smart-looking little man, seated in a kind of glass-case, seriously occupied in turning over the leaves of a book in which were written the names of all visi-

tors to the castle. And there, indeed, he might sit
and wait for a long while, without having much to
write in it, for the barred gate was a hindrance to
every one.

To this little man, who was very gaily and neatly
dressed, and still wore the old-fashioned powdered
*queue,* our young gentleman commenced bowing and
scraping all the way as he advanced toward him;
and then, with becoming deference, addressed him
with, " Be so good as to tell me who lives in this
beautiful castle?"

"Nobody!" answered the little man, with a con-
temptuous glance at the diminutive questioner,
whose poverty-stricken garments were certainly not
very suitable in the vicinity of such a wonderful castle. And having given this short, unfriendly answer, went on with his book as seriously as if he had
the weightiest affairs to settle.

" So, then, I am to live here," thought our little
one in much astonishment. " Well, I can make
myself very happy, although I should certainly like
to know who it is who is so kindly disposed toward
me."

And with this he passed quietly by the doorkeeper's glass lodge, without causing him to look up
from his book, and ascended the broad marble steps,
upon each side of which stood beautiful statues as
large as life. Thinking that they were a number
of men and women also living in the spacious castle,

he took off his hat to every one as he passed, and felt very angry that they did not acknowledge his politeness. He next entered a splendid saloon, the floor of which was smooth and polished as a mirror, and our friend soon began to slide about right and left.

Being afraid of falling, he seated himself in a softly-padded rocking-chair; but scarcely had he sat down than it began to swing backward and forward, so that the poor child was almost sea-sick, and seized hold of a cord hanging down the side of the wall. All at once the clear sound of a bell rang through the room, and servants with bewildered faces rushed in from the three doors, breathlessly inquiring "who had rung the bell?"

As soon as they caught sight of the equally astonished boy in his shabby clothes, whose chair was still rocking backward and forward, with a face looking green, yellow, and all colors, they all rushed angrily upon him, and threatened to beat him out of the castle for disturbing their repose.

"What do you want with me, then?" asked the little one, frankly. "I am to live in this castle, and have therefore a right to be here. Only just ask the porter—he will tell you so. I am called Nobody, and you may as well bring me something to eat, for I am hungry."

The attendants ran down to inquire if they were really to wait upon Nobody, and if the cook was to cook for Nobody.

"Of course," said the little man, with great dignity. "So long as you are in this castle you will serve Nobody as your gracious master, and the cook shall cook for Nobody. Whoever acts in opposition to this command will be dismissed on the spot."

So the servants went back shaking their heads, and were now as humble and subservient to the little fellow as they had before been rude and angry. First of all he made them help him out of the rocking-chair, and then they brought him the most dainty dishes they could find; for the porter had told them, you know, that they were to serve Nobody as their gracious master; and none of them wished to disobey this order, for fear of losing a good place.

Their master rarely came to the castle more than once in the course of years. "There must be something singular about this child," they said to each other, and treated the little visitor as if he had been a prince. He ate well, drank well, and finished with sleeping well in his silken bed.

The next morning the servants brought him a tailor, who inquired most deferentially whether he might make him some new clothes. He was very glad to give him permission, and allowed Master Threadpaper to measure him as much as he liked for coat and frock-coat, waistcoat, and trowsers and dressing-gown.

It was not very long before he brought with him

a whole stock of clothes from his warehouse, all of so fine a quality, and so beautiful, that our hero scarcely recognized himself when he looked at himself in the mirror.

But next came a bad moment for the lucky one, for Master Threadpaper seemed to expect payment. "Nobody has money now—Nobody will pay me," said he, turning to the servants ; but the little one heard it well, and all at once the lofty and spacious saloon became too small for him. " Oh, if I were but once away from here !" thought he ; and before any one in the castle had noticed it, he had crept down the wide marble steps, past the doorkeeper, who, not recognizing the well-dressed boy, politely took off his hat to him, and inquired his name, which he entered in his book with the utmost gravity.

Meanwhile the little one stole cautiously through the garden, over the iron gate, and, thanks to his tolerably swift feet, was soon at a distance from the wonderful castle. No sooner did he feel safe, than he began to reflect upon what he should do next. "Ah," thought he, "if that tailor had never made his appearance, I might have remained in that lovely castle for the rest of my life !"

Having reached a strange village, he paused outside the second house, and listened :

" M-o-u-s-e—mouse ; h-o-u-s-e—house !" was echoed through the open windows from a room full of children.

"Eh! that must be a school," thought the boy; and it occurred to him that his father had often said that everybody must go to school who meant to be of any use in the world. So he took heart, and went in. He tapped modestly at the door, and the school-master sent a child to see who it was, and what was wanted.

"Mr. Schoolmaster, Nobody is outside," was the answer brought back.

"Well, then, sit down quietly in your place," said the master, and continued teaching the little ones upon the phonetic system.

Our young friend, meanwhile, stood outside in the passage, waiting and waiting.

At last the child who had returned to his form, where the master bade him, ventured to say, "With your leave, teacher, Nobody wishes to come to school."

The schoolmaster was one of the hasty kind; and as he put quite another construction upon the child's words to what had been intended, he let his birch-rod fall with tolerable weight upon the back and shoulders of the little speaker.

Our little one outside in the passage lost almost all desire for a visit to the school, and yet he would have been glad to learn something; so he took courage, went into the school-room, represented his wish to the master, and told him his name.

"Well, we will try for once how we can get on

together," answered the schoolmaster, with some kindness; just sit down below upon that form, and give **all your attention** to what is going on at first."

The boy did as he was **ordered, and** looked at the great picture-alphabet with all attention, **but without** understanding anything **about it.** It did not last **very long, for the** children began pelting each other with unripe fruit, and laughing, as soon **as the school-master had** turned **his back** upon them.

He came angrily to the table where the culprits were sitting.

" Who has been throwing fruit ? Who has been laughing ?" asked he sternly, with a threatening frown.

" Nobody !" exclaimed **six or eight** voices **with one mouth ; and the schoolmaster, without** more **ado,** seized our frightened little one by the ears, and shook him severely, **as he** pushed him somewhat roughly out of the room.

" That was soon settled," thought the maligned one, as he dried his eyes, and slunk away sadly.

He came to a heap of rubbish, where several children were playing. He sat down, and joined them in building cellars and vaults, steps and fountains. They were all very merry and happy together, when an ugly old woman suddenly came hobbling out of the neighboring cottage before which the children were playing, with a crutch in her hand, and calling out as she drew near—" Only just wait, you naughty

children, you shall not mess about with that sand
for nothing. I will teach you to **play** before other
people's doors."

So saying, she stopped, swinging **her crutch right**
before the children, who would gladly have run out
of her way.

"Ah! Mother Hartman, we will not play any
more on your dust-heap—we beg of you to beat Nobody."

The poor little fellow **did not know why it was**
that these children **with whom he had just** been
playing **so merrily** had begged **the old woman to**
beat him. **He was ready to cry at their** great **un-**
kindness; and more sadly **than ever he went on his**
road through the village in which he had been so
badly treated.

In the fields beyond he laid himself down, under
a thorn-hedge, tired and hungry, but without the
courage to speak to any one, or beg for anything;
so he sat under the great branches, and wept bitterly.

**A great many people were busy in** the fields, hay-
making; they sang and joked, and were **very** merry
over their work, without noticing **the child.** All at
**once,** along the high road, came a horseman with
slackened rein. He dismounted, and coming into
the meadow where the people were singing, he held
his horse while inquiring if they had chanced to find
a pocket-book on the road.

"I lost it an hour ago, somewhere about here, and
**there are** some very important papers in it."

"Nobody had seen a pocket-book, Nobody had picked it up," the honest country people declared, and leaving their **work, set** about helping the rider to **look for it.**

Our little friend **under the** hawthorn thought that **they** were searching **for him, and crept** eagerly into the ditch till they could no longer see him. **He did** not know how he should produce the **pocket-book, however gladly he** would have **done so.**

**It** was already getting dark, and **his** tired feet could scarcely bear him from the spot. At last he reached a lonely farm-house, where he intended begging a piece of bread and a night's lodging. As he tremblingly stepped into the farm-yard, he heard an angry dispute **from the ground-floor of** the dwelling. **It was a woman's voice entreating :**

"Do **not** go **to the** public-house again, my **dear** husband ; things are bad enough without that. **We** have so many debts, and you gamble away our last penny at the card-table. Do but think of me and your children !"

The husband answered, angrily :

"I make no promises, and will **put** up with no reproaches. Nobody will help me ! Nobody will pay my debts !"

Our little one waited no longer. He ran away as fast as he could, farther and farther, till **he** came to a dark **wood—to the** birds and squirrels, to the cockchafers and tree-frogs, **who** did not know his name. There he sits to-day—ever—no longer daring to come among men. You have only to go some day and look ; you will find Nobody there !

---

## TURKISH TITLES.

"THE Sublime Porte" is the official title of the Government of the Ottoman Empire, and not the title of any officer of the Government, as many suppose it to be.

The Ottoman Emperor is called Sultan, or Grand Sultan, or Grand Seignior, according to the fancy of the person speaking or writing.

Pacha is the Governor of a province, and according to the importance of his province, he is distinguished by one, or two, or three tails. A Pacha with three tails has the power to punish with death any agent whom he employs, or any individual who seems to threaten the general safety.

Bey is a sub-governor under the Pacha.

The Divan is the Council of State, and consists of the principal ministers.

Cadi, is a sort of judge or justice of the peace. To order the bastinado on common people, to impose a fine on a rich Greek or European, to condemn a thief to be hanged, is about all the duty of an ordinary Cadi.

## THE OLD ENGLISH VILLAGE PASTOR.

" E'en children followed with endearing smile,
And plucked his gown, to share the good man's smile."

SUCH was the village pastor in England, who wore a long black robe or gown, and white linen bands about his neck, when he was in the church.

A poet has told us of one of these who lived many years ago. Everybody loved him ; he listened to everybody's troubles, and always helped them if he could ; and considered himself *rich* with "forty pounds a year," (not far from two hundred dollars.) All the poor knew his house, and were sure of being treated kindly there.

How pleasant to see the children, as he comes out of the church door, gather around him and get hold of his hand for love to him, for often he would draw them to his knee and his lap for pleasant talk ! Years and years he lived in the same place—scarcely ever thought of going away, but only of being and doing good. You will say this is being like your own pastors, for I trust you have all good ones.

In this country, many years ago, they lived longer in the same place than they do now. Great-great-grandmothers could tell you of pastors or ministers who lived through three generations in the same place. One village pastor in New England (and many did the same) married the daughter (performed the marriage ceremony) of one of his people ; then baptized *her* child ; then married *her* (the child, when grown,) and baptized *her* child—three generations of them. That was before everybody went " West."

Fathers, and children, and grandchildren all stayed in one place, as well as the pastor, in those times.

The village schoolmaster was next to the pastor in importance. He used in old times to dress very carefully, carried a cane, and was very dignified in his manners. When, in his walks, he came where some who were his pupils a year or two ago, but now grown up and enjoying pastimes in the fields, or chatting under the hawthorn or elm-tree, he would make the most stately bow, and inquire after the health of Emily and Julius, and so on.  Then the young woman, Emily, would blush and drop her eyes, with the old feeling that she used to have, in the presence of "the master," who in those days used

> "Words of learned length, and thundering sound."

It is all right to have a very great respect for teachers, and every rule they make should be implicitly obeyed ; for a good teacher will make none but good ones.

Mr. Livingstone, one of these schoolmasters with the "cocked hat," was a very kind-hearted man, but very *strict* in his school.  He always *punished* any misbehavior among his pupils in a way of his own.

One day Letty Meed bent her head upon her desk, and ate from some fruit, during school hours ; this, of course, was misconduct.  Mr. Livingstone was sitting upon a high seat, quite across the room, listening to a recitation.  Without looking toward Letty, or even lifting his eyes from his text-book, he said distinctly—O how distinctly—Letty thought every word rang :

"You remind me of the ostrich, when she is frightened ; she sticketh her head in the wall, and thinketh she is secure."

That was every word he said ; he spoke no name.  Then he went on with the class recitation.  Letty

smarted as if under a whip ; and as she lifted her
scarlet face, every scholar saw that she was the cul-
prit—her cheeks made the confession ; and you may
be sure she never needed Mr. Livingstone's reprie-
mand again.

THE PASTOR LISTENING TO THE NEWS.

LIZZIE IN THE GARDEN.

## A WARNING.

THERE was once a little girl named Lizzy, who had a habit of disobeying her mother, and, as she was very careless, she did many mischievous things.

In consequence of all this, the mother had given her many serious lessons, and had warned her of the dangers of her misconduct. But Lizzy was very self-willed, and was resolved to have her own way. Alas! how severely was she punished for her folly and disobedience!

One day Lizzy was playing with some of her little friends, and in order to carry on the play, she lighted a candle. This had been positively forbidden by her mother, for several accidents had happened in consequence of Lizzy's playing with fire. However, the undutiful child would follow her own wishes. Soon after she had lighted the candle, she thought she heard her mother's step. She therefore set the candle behind the bed, to keep it out of sight.

After a while she forgot the light, and went into the garden with her young companions. What was her horror, soon after, to hear the cry of fire, and to feel sure that the candle was the cause of it! She rushed to the house, but all was a scene of terror and confusion. Her mother and little sister had scarce time to escape from the flames.

The house was indeed reduced to ashes, and Lizzy's father and mother, for some years, had many cares and sufferings in consequence of the loss of their home. This was a terrible lesson to Lizzy, and indeed it ought to be a warning to all thoughtless and undutiful children. Fathers and mothers are made the guardians of their offspring by God himself, and these are told by the solemn commandment, to honor and obey their parents.

Indeed, obedience to parents ought not to be felt as a duty only : no child's heart is right till it loves obedience, and finds a high pleasure and enjoyment in fulfilling the injunctions and wishes of those who have brought it into life.